STUCK ON You

4

A NOVEL BY

SUNNY GIOVANNI

ACKNOWLEDGEMENTS

I have a very long list of incredible readers, yet I don't have the capacity to single you out, because I might forget someone and they might wind up mad at me over it. So, THANK YOU ALL FOR THE CONTINUED SUPPORT AND LOVE! You know you're the best. Your numbers seem to grow with each and every release, and you make me one happy author!

Porscha Sterling and Quiana Nicole, you are two hard working women that I'm lucky to work with... when I'm not pestering you for no reason at all. With each release, no matter the bumps in the road, if there are any, you two ladies smooth it out and get it done with ease. What can I say? I guess that's just what royals do.

Rooooob! Robin Conner, you have become one of my Ace Boons, and I have to say that checking my inbox every day for the last few months has been an adventure. If any normal person were to hack our accounts and tried to keep up without conversations, they would truly end up lost and scratching their heads. Thank you for being a vociferous weirdo like me. I'm not alone! Keep droppin' heat like you've been doing. I'm proud of you!

Keish Andrea and Vaneecia, y'all are the truth. What I learned from you is to never judge a book by its cover, and that's only because y'all look innocent, but you keep me laughing until I'm crying. You two are amazing young women in your prime. I can see you soaring further and wallowing in your continued success. Salute!

Larissa, Misty, both Jasmines, Kendra Rainey and Shavekia, you are my A-1's. I love your honesty and your humor. Without you gals, I might have a limp in my step. Remain the goddesses you are and continue to prosper through all of the hardships and rainy days. I love you!

My family and distant friends, I love you. There's no disputing that. I keep you all close for a reason. That's why I praise you when I can or give you comfort. Thank you so much for all that you've done for me. You are appreciated.

SOUNDTRACK

"Fool in Love" – **Rihanna**

"Jealous" – **Labrinth**

"Fall For You" – **Leela James**

"Side Effect of You" – **Fantasia**

"Brave" – **Jhene Aiko**

"The Way" – **Kehlani & Chance the Rapper**

"XO" – **Beyoncé**

"Ashley" – **Big Sean & Miguel**

"Touch Me" – **Chris Brown & Sevyn Streeter**

"You" – **Jesse Powell**

PROLOGUE

When We Were Young

Twelve Years Ago…

$\mathcal{T}$he classroom was all abuzz with students flocking in from their previous classes. Fortunately, Mandy, Rich, Shane, and Cherie all had Home Economics together. For their end of semester projects, they had a whole six weeks to create a life with their partner. That included a monthly budget, a career choice, a home with a separate collage of the interior designs, and they all had a choice of having a family. Today, they were given the first thirty minutes out of the two hours of the period to wrap up their projects before they had to present.

Rich and Mandy, sitting at the island in front of Shane and Cherie's, were already fussing as soon as they dropped their book bags. Cherie lightly giggled as she pasted the edge of her cutout of the Jaguar she wanted. Shane slid up next to her just before the bell rang, feasting his eyes on it. The luxury sports car was to die for, and he loved the color of it.

"That's what you want?" he asked her, startling her in the process.

Cherie gasped and looked back at him with a smile. "Of course it's what I want. Why else would I put it on the board?"

"I don't know any twelve-year-old girl who wants a Jag... but if that's what my little woman wants, then—"

"Man, shut up!" Rich yelled at him. "You always got to be a show-off."

"You shut up!" Mandy worked her neck at him. "You got me a Buick!"

"Ain't nothin' wrong with a Buick, girl."

"It is when it's from 1982! And it's a two door! How are we supposed to put the babies' car seats in that? Three of them, Rich?"

"You're the one who wanted triplets! All I had to do was point and shoot. No money involved."

"*Money?*"

"Nope. I budgeted. That was part of the assignment. We couldn't afford the gas from our current time period *and* an SUV. You know damn well that after September 11th, Bush raised the gas prices. Why you think my mama don't drive her car?"

"Because her license was *revoked.*"

Rich sucked his teeth as he waved her off. "Minor detail."

"Well, I'm fortunate that Shane decided to obtain his Master's in Architectural Designs," Cherie gushed. She wrapped her arms around his neck, resting her cheek against his chest. "Not only does he earn a six-figure salary in a year, but with the way he allows me to be an entrepreneur, I have plenty of fun money in between his commission and monthly earnings."

"If y'all needed some dough, y'all could've just asked us." Shane winked at Rich.

Rich and Mandy looked at each other, then back at them. "Fuck y'all!" they yelled in unison.

"Okay, everyone! Simmer down!" Mrs. Carson told them all from the front of the room. She adjusted her small, rectangular specs so that she could take roll mentally. "We'll be starting in alphabetical order this afternoon. The first thing you're going to present will be your engagements and weddings. Then, we'll take everything else from there. What you should be working on now are your visuals. If I see anything with stick figures on it or something that doesn't fashionably hang from your boards, that will be an automatic failure. Are we clear?"

"Yes, Mrs. Carson," her students dryly sang.

"Good. Now come, come, my little seventh graders. There is much more to experience today."

Mandy gave Rich the middle finger before she got to work on finishing up their visual for the interior of their home.

Cherie had already gotten her and Shane's visuals in order, and Shane was okay with it. He was there with her every day and each time she placed a clipping in her binder. Some of her favorite ideas, she put into the home of her choosing. It would be the home that Shane built for her.

"Oh, did you see my ideas for our wedding?" Cherie asked happily while Shane took his seat.

"Oh, you mean the gown you chose that reminded you oh so much of Belle's from *Beauty and the Beast*? And the horse-drawn carriage for when we leave the castle? Oh, and the reception! How it's themed differently from the actual wedding itself because you want each table with a different Disney theme?"

"Aww!" she gushed. "You do pay attention to me."

"Of course I do. Now, what about these kids?"

"Now, you know we're going to have to wait until I get all of my kicks out of life before we have kids."

"Rie, we're five years into our marriage, according to this project, and you're getting ready to open a resort and spa, which I helped to design and build. We're only supposed to do the first five years, but Rich and Mandy over there with triplets already. What about the two sets of twins you wanted? Especially with all different colored eyes?"

Cherie started to say something but was interrupted by Rich.

"That's just impossible. Cherie, you're asking for too much. He already gave you a resort, and now you want him to skeet all over the place."

"Language!" Mrs. Carson yelled within a hiss.

"My bad, Mrs. C! I'm just saying. The girl wants her kids to obviously wear contacts or something."

Shane leaned over when he saw the scowl on Cherie's face. He whispered to her, "If you want that wedding, the house, the kids, the resort, and the Jag... *none* of it is impossible, Rie." Then, he pecked her cheek.

He always knew how to make her smile. To Cherie, Shane was the best. No man would ever be like him, and she knew so. Whoever would try to date her would have some pretty big shoes to fill. However, she imagined their project wedding as something that would be their own one day.

Shane looked around the room that was reminiscent of a large kitchen, at all the happy faces— some not so happy because they weren't done with their projects— and stopped at the only person who didn't have a partner. She was the fat kid in class, and even worse, she was the deacon's daughter. They all thought that she was a holy roller, so they avoided her trying to throw the bible in their faces, if she was even that kind of person. No one knew because they let her father's position in the pulpit get the better of them. Not only that, but no twelve-year-old boy wanted to even think of marrying a fat girl. April Patterson sat alone, doodling on a piece of white paper. She was obviously done with her assignment, and she seemed as content as can be. Shane felt a little pity for her since the class was uneven. There was even a couple— a best friend duo— who prepared a lesbian ceremony and who planned on educating them all on acceptance for the LGBT community. He would've thought that someone would've done that with April, yet it didn't seem to bother her.

"Shane, can we release doves after our ceremony?" Cherie asked as she pulled away. "You know, like after we come out of the church doors? It'll be so pretty! Plus, I saw a pretty dove in a magazine that I clipped out, and I want to use it."

Shane lightly shrugged. "If that's what my little woman wants."

5

CHAPTER ONE

I Need An Answer

After all of the planning and all of the photos and smiles, it was time to take their vows. Shane's heart rate was through the roof. All of the mistakes he made, all of the days he wasted, and possibly having the perfect mother figure for his daughter should've come into play. He hadn't realized that he had been coasting. Terry helped to remind him of that after his early morning visit. Terry reminded him of how far one was willing to go for Cherie. What he thought was love and a carefree life was just him coasting. The feeling of nausea crept back up on him when the pastor asked the dreaded question that most people didn't want to hear out of fear that someone would stand in the way of their happiness. Shane expected Terry to be standing at the back of the church with a smirk on his face at Shane's next move because he was getting married and it was to Cherie.

"If anyone has a reason for these two not to wed, speak now or forever hold your peace."

Shane kept his eyes on April's until hers diverted. She looked over at Cherie on her side of the church.

Cherie, in turn, tilted her head with furrowed brows. *What in the hell is she about to do?*

Slowly, April took a sloppy step back and raised her hand to oppose their union.

Shane closed his eyes as the crowd erupted in gasps. Inside, he was breathing a sigh of relief that he wasn't the only one to feel that their union would've been a mistake.

"Speak your peace," the pastor prompted her.

April donned a small smile, lifted herself on the tips of her toes, and then whispered in Shane's ear. Her reasoning wasn't anyone else's business. "You still love her," she told him. "This has gone absolutely too far, and the both of us know so. She should be standing here, not me. I love you, Shane, but I don't love you enough for you to live a lie. Especially with me. Now please tell these people that they can still go to the reception. I'm hungry, and I could use a few drinks." She settled in her heels after giving him a peck on the cheek. She turned to the audience, explaining, "I want to thank De'Shane for showing me the greater side of love, and for letting me experience what a good man he's been… but he and I both know that I'm not the one who's supposed to be standing here."

"*She found her balls,*" Cherie said to herself.

"Right," Shane sided with her. "Now, if you all could please join us in the reception hall so we all can get some food and drinks in our system. We both would greatly appreciate you."

April smiled at him as he took her hand into his and kissed the top of it. The two took their walk down the aisle, yet April had to stop on the row where Cherie sat. When she stood, April handed her the bouquet from her hands, then wrapped Cherie up inside a tight embrace.

"You better claim him before someone who isn't understanding does it," she whispered. "Come on, girl. I know you got it in you."

Cherie couldn't even look at Shane in that moment. She knew that what April was saying was true. How much more time were they going to waste by running from one another?

———————

Cherie had to take some time to straighten her makeup in the restroom after she cried her eyes out in the stall. It was almost too late, yet again, and there was almost nothing that she could've done about it. Once she reached the reception hall, the DJ had "Booty-Whop" by Big Freedia blaring from the speakers. She couldn't believe how nasty some people were getting on the dancefloor, but she could've imagined since she spent some of her childhood in New Orleans and witnessed how grungy they could be. April's side of the family was in the building after receiving word that they jumped straight to the reception. Cherie had to sneer at them.

"Oh, Cherie!" April called over the music.

She had changed into the dress that she found for the reception only, and Cherie had to admire her in it for a moment. She looked dashing in her Make Way maxi dress. Stretchy, floral lace peeked through to a beige lining, constructing a plunging neckline fortified by a hidden V bar for April's shape. Sheer chiffon fell from the natural waistline, opening into a full-length slit on the right side to expose a little leg. The way April's hair was pulled up into a bun, it all flowed effortlessly. Cherie almost felt guilty for ruining this moment for the woman.

April wore no shoes when she stumbled toward her, and Cherie noticed. Still, she latched on to Cherie's arm and slurred, "I heard that you like mango-ritas. The bartender is doing a very amazing job over there. He dilutes *nothing*."

Cherie had to turn her head away when getting a very good whiff of the Jose Cuervo on her breath.

"You should go and get a few."

"No, it's okay. I think maybe you've had too much."

"Nuh-uh. This is practically the only wedding I'm ever gonna get, so I have to live it up while I can. And speaking of living." She searched around the room for a moment before she found Shane dancing with a random girl. "Excuse me for a moment. Don't go anywhere... and keep looking this beautiful. I'll be right back. You workin' it, girl."

Cherie knew that April was drunk with her lazy words and her overly-animated speech to try and cover it up... but it only made her wonder how long she had been crying alone in the stall to begin with.

Shortly after leaving, April came marching right back to her. She didn't stop, however. She grabbed Cherie tightly by the hand and continued her journey out of the hall and into the corridor. She hadn't known where she was going, but she knew she was taking them somewhere. She had her answer when she saw an open closet door. It was the janitor's closet. She let them go, grabbed a mop out, and shoved the two inside.

"What the fuck?" Cherie screamed, almost stumbling over her heels.

"April!" Shane bellowed.

She successfully shut the door and lodged the handle of the mop inside the hole of the square-shaped handle. With her back to it, she promised, "You're not coming out until you talk to each other, and be honest."

"April, this is crazy!" Shane shouted. "Let us out of here! You wanted us to talk, and we've done that!"

"You were hiding things… you… you… *hiderers!*"

"April, honey," Cherie called sweetly. "You're just a little loaded. Shane and I are fine."

"No, you're not! You can't even lie to *me* now. The both of you were willing to hide and run from each other so much that you almost let me and Shane live a lie for the rest of our lives. Oh, but I'm the one that's crazy? And for the record… I'm not a little loaded. I'm *a lot* of loaded. So while I enjoy my liquor, you two talk amongst yourselves—"

"What the hell are you doing?" Nicola asked after rounding the corner from the restroom.

"You mind your own business, bitch." April might've been angry, but it was more than clear that she was drunk off her ass. She was a lightweight and didn't even know it. "Why don't you get out of here and go cuddle up with your husband who has eyes for everyone else but you. And don't you judge me. At least *my* wedding actually meant something."

"You need to calm down."

"How about you fuck off and tell Tucker that my niece isn't his. Hmm? You wanna do that, Nicola?"

"You are drunk and don't know what you're saying."

"Well… you're sober and still fucking *stupid*. Now get out of here and enjoy Shane's money. At least he makes some anyway."

Nicola rolled her eyes and trotted along, even though she had been basically read to hell by her younger sister.

April knocked on the door with her back still to it. "You still in there?"

Shane covered his face as Cherie dropped hers. "Of course we're still in here," he told her politely. "You have us locked in, sweetie."

Slowly, April slid to the floor in her designer gown, sitting on her legs. "Now tell each other. Shane, tell her how badly you've wanted her to come back as the best friend that you had, but she's changed. You feel foolish because she doesn't necessarily need you, and that you feel that she doesn't see all of what you've done for her. Go on."

He looked over at Cherie in the dimly lit room, not sure how to express the truths that he hadn't known were so evident.

"And, Cherie… girl, I love your damn dress… but tell Shane how long you've been waiting for him to be the best friend that was willing to do anything for you, but you still partly hate him for not coming to look for you in the first place. Tell him how scared you've been. Tell him how scared you were to break free, but you came back and found him with someone else."

Cherie stared back at him with a frown. The saying that a drunk man will tell no tales was true. In April's case, it was a drunk woman.

"God, why is it so hard for you two to see that nobody will ever be able to love either of you completely because you're still holding on to each other? And while it's not a bad thing, the good part about it is that you two are soulmates. The bad part is that you're two consenting adults who are running away from each other but holding each other prisoner. When two souls combine, they come together and… and… and do *souly* stuff. But you won't let your souls do shit, and that's why you're both hurt, angry, confused, and lying like hell to each other and yourselves."

Neither of them could fight it. What she was saying was true. It took someone who hadn't known them to do something crazy like this, just for them to see it.

"Come on, damn you," she whined. "How many more of us are going to have to sacrifice real love, or the chance at it, for the lack thereof, just because the both of you are stubborn like hell and are being foolish? How many more of us are you going to use as duplicates or replacements?"

"April, baby—" Shane started but was abruptly cut off.

"No, fuck that! It stops here! It stops right here! Now I may not be much of a courageous person, but I have to grab my testicles with both hands today."

A cousin of Shane's was passing her in the hall when he stopped at looked down at the woman who was now sitting with her legs agape. Thank God she was wearing bloomers underneath her dress or else he would've seen her sheer thong underneath. He was searching for her mentioned testicles when she realized he was staring.

"What the fuck are you staring at?" she yelled at him. "Get the fuck out of here! We're trying to have a moment here!"

"There's no one here," he reasoned.

"Will you leave us alone?" she screamed. "Find something to do, rudeness!"

Frightful, he scurried away, making a mental note to tell his uncle's wife that the woman his cousin almost married was sitting and speaking to herself.

"Talk!" Weakly, she banged on the door, then rested the back of her head against it.

"Cherie," Shane started.

"No, let me," she stopped him.

He nodded and backed into the corner to let her take the conversation.

"I'm sorry. I'm sorry for putting us through this—"

Using his impressive wingspan, Shane reached out for Cherie's waist and latched onto it, snatching her right out of a sentence. She lightly gasped when her body smashed into his. Cherie searched through his eyes as she had always done and found that there was nothing she could say. They were on the same page. No words could express how stupid either of them had been, or how stubborn they had been to let things get this far.

"What are we going to do about April?" Cherie mumbled.

"I'll have Rich take her to the honeymoon suite we got."

"And the guests?"

"Let them party. After all, it's still a celebration."

"Of?"

"How a drunk woman made a serious sacrifice today, and then made two stupid people wise the hell up before it was too late."

"And what are we supposed to say to her, Shane?" Cherie began to panic. "This seems kind of wrong, doesn't it? I mean, she just had her dream wedding, and then—"

"Let me worry about that, alright? No worries, no stress. I got us. Haven't I always?"

"Yea, but she—"

"April will be fine. I promise."

"Are you sure?"

"Very sure of it."

"The bigger question is… how the hell do we get out of here?"

He chuckled, even though his thoughts were on more than April. He swallowed the urge to tell Cherie that Terry visited him last night and that he's possibly still in Richmond somewhere.

CHAPTER TWO

Go To Work

Shane had gotten out of his Hummer, focused as he had ever been. Miracle was starting her first day of daycare, and it took for his sisters and Cherie to remind him that she would be okay. Before his surgery, he would've been adamant about taking her out of there, but now he had a little more trust. However, he didn't have trust for gutter rats. At four in the morning, he rolled over to his phone vibrating across his nightstand. A few of his workers were in an uproar about finding out that there was a thief amongst the dealers. He told them to keep it cool and to remain as calm as possible. Everyone had been used to Shane being so cool and tight-lipped about everything, yet no one expected him to sound so okay with the situation. They should've known better.

The God didn't need a key to enter the rundown house on the corner. After he parked in the driveway, he walked right through the front door, hearing Rich cackle and talk with someone. He feasted his eyes upon a tall and buff man who was only wearing a muscle shirt and jeans.

"Homie, Shane, have you met… uhh?" Rich pointed to the man with his thumb.

"Buckwild," the man introduced himself.

"Yea, this is *him*."

The man only thought that he was being introduced to the boss. After years of seeing Apollo handle his employees, Shane knew that with all the things that were changing in his life that this couldn't be one of them.

"Buckwild, huh?" Shane stroked his goatee with his eyes on the amused man who had developed sticky fingers in the absence of the boss.

"Yea, that's me," he replied with a laugh.

Little did he know, those would be the very last words that he would ever speak again. Shane quickly drew his piece and fired off one silent shot, landing right between Buckwild's eyes.

Others who were passing or working didn't even have time to gasp when his body hit the floor.

Shane stood over him, tapping the nose of his gun against his leg. The diamonds on the band of his wristwatch gleamed in the sunlight that seeped in through tattered curtains that hang loosely over the single window in the living room.

"Damn, Shane," Rich said lowly, shoveling peanuts from the palm of his hand into his mouth. "You shot that nigga."

Shane didn't return a lyric or a mumble.

"Somebody come and clean this mess up!" Rich ordered with a

full mouth. "They know damn well not to steal from you."

"Was he new?" someone asked in the distance.

"I think he was. But shit, this is the jungle. He just got mauled."

By the time Rich looked up, Shane was already out of the front door and was getting into his SUV.

He smirked, thinking that Shane had taken his advice of thinking for himself for a change. "Welcome back, my brotha. Welcome back."

––––––––––

Keeping to his time, Shane picked up money, went over inventory, then stopped at a diner for lunch. With his trusty phone attached to his hand, he searched for florists so that he could have something delivered with the quickness. Then, he was off to the market to grab steaks and shrimp, Miracle's teething cookies, fruits, and whatever veggies he was going to cook for the night. He only had another hour before he had to retrieve Miracle from daycare, so he had to throw his dinner on low so that he could finish running around. When he was with Miracle, that was just it. His daughter meant more to him than money, a job, or anyone else for that matter. Tonight, however, he was planning to put her to bed early. Daddy had some things that he had to sew together and mend.

On the way to Rainbow's Children's Day Center, Shane received a call from Rich. He frowned at it, hoping that his best friend could handle whatever issues that might have arose since he left the trap earlier.

"What it is?" Shane answered.

"Bruh, you missed almost ten grand," Rich informed him. "You alright?"

"What?" Shane frowned. There was no way that he could've missed something. He was Shane the God. There was no way.

"Mechanicsville. Them boys called and said that you didn't stop through. I checked with the White dudes in Midlothian, and they said you were on time."

"I… I…" Shane shut his eyes tight at a stop light to get his words together. He didn't like to forget. Even worse, he didn't like to not be on time or in control.

"Listen, bro. The doctors said that it would take you some time to get back to normal. It's no biggie. It was an honest mistake. I done already sent Lyssa out there to cop it for you."

"No! You call her and tell her to stand down!"

"Shane, bro, we got you. We know that it's going to take some time, alright. It's nothing to be ashamed of. And listen to this. How about me and Lyssa work the ground for you, and you just keep up with the inventory and shit? Huh? Even Apollo didn't do everything by himself. It's only been nine months since the surgery. You can't expect to be a hunnit percent by now."

"Rich, I'm not supposed to fall, bruh!"

"Yea, but it's life. You know we ain't gon' let you fall. Just look at it like this: You tripped a little bit and we caught you before you stumbled. That's what friends are for. Now go and get my niece and don't forget how to get back home, motherfucker."

"Whatever." Though Shane laughed it off, he wasn't at all happy with his work or his lack of memory.

———————

Cherie showed up to the modern townhome as excited as she wanted to be. She hadn't been in the home that was built for her since Shane was released from the Pavilion. She stopped and checked her hair in the mirror before heading inside of the garage. Once again, she changed her color. She was a jet black with classy white streaks. Thanks to Quita, her hair was freshly done. All she was told this morning, before heading off to a meeting with Erykah, was that she was expected at the house. Shane texted her the time and let her know that she knew damn well which house he was talking about.

It was nearing eight when she used her thumbprint to get into the home. It sat so still and quiet that it almost frightened her. The smell in the air, on the other hand, beckoned for her to lift the lids of the pots on the stove. Cautiously, she approached them, trying to guess what was in each of them. Before she could lay a hand on the first lid, the doorbell rang, startling the sneaky woman. She shut her eyes and huffed. She should've known not to be sneaky in her own home.

Cherie waited for a moment to see if Shane would come galloping down the steps. When he didn't, she scurried to the door in her heels to see what visitor he could've had at this time of night.

A uniformed man stood there with a full bouquet of red chrysanthemums and white carnations, with bonds of purple hyacinth in the mix. Instantly, a smile blossomed onto Cherie's face.

"Mon Cherie Anton?" the man asked her.

Cherie giggled as she playfully rolled her eyes. "That's me."

"These are for you. Have a goodnight."

She accepted her bouquet, feeling the weight of the world lift momentarily. Lightly, she swayed back into the kitchen with her vase in her hand, admiring her lush gift. She was so caught up into staring at them and loving the smell that she hadn't heard Shane gallop down the steps or enter the kitchen. The only thing to bring her out of her trance was hearing the top behind her clang onto the pot. She jolted and turned around in her heels to see him standing there with the tip of his thumb in his mouth. He was sucking the juice of his boiled Cajun shrimp off his finger.

Cherie started to say something, but she was caught between a rock and a hard place. In her case, she was stuck between wanting to pull his long dreads, stroke his bare arm that stuck out from his black muscle shirt, or lick the tattoo that lined his collarbone.

Shane's thick lips stretched into a devilish smirk. Slowly, he lifted the top once again, but this time he snagged a piece of shrimp, dangling it in front of her face. "Come on, Rie. You know you want to try it."

She leaned forward and parted her cherry red lips.

Being an asshole, Shane snatched it back. He dropped the shrimp into his mouth, then chewed it with a smile on his face.

"Ass!" Cherie shrieked.

"It's almost done," he chuckled as he searched under the bar for his sauté pan.

"Look at you," she teased with a grin. "Looking like you know what you're doing."

"Girl, please. My mama never cooked, remember? Of course, I know what I'm doing."

"Mmhhmm. I'm pretty sure you had to have a fire extinguisher somewhere in the kitchen with you."

"Please. And because I was on a very strict diet at my old man's, I had to learn how to make my own meals. The chef wasn't always going to be there. It was either learn or starve. You think the almighty Apollo didn't cook his own food? You would be sadly mistaken, just like everybody else who assumed that."

Cherie rolled her eyes again as she hopped up on the island to watch him work his magic.

Shane drained the shrimp in the sink, then tossed it into the pan that he had already drizzled olive oil in. Cherie was impressed by how he worked the handle of the pan. The glitch in his muscle as he moved it back and forth somehow gave her the wanting of him plunging his fingers inside of her with as much force and vigor.

"Hope you like Corona."

"Hmm?" She snapped out of her nasty thought for only a millisecond to see him pour a fourth of a bottle of beer over the shrimp and seasoning. She was so busy daydreaming that she hadn't seen him sprinkle paprika, chives, and sea salt into the pan.

Shane chuckled at her as he found their plates in the cupboards.

"Where's Miracle?" she inquired.

"Sleeping. Thanks to Melatonin, she's resting her pretty little head."

23

"You drugged her?"

"Don't say it like that." He then shoveled rice out of a small pot onto their square-shaped plates on the countertop, topping it off with his Ragin' Cajun shrimp. Lastly, he took the top off of a cast-iron skillet to reveal the juiciest steaks Cherie had ever seen.

Like a gentleman, he took their plates to the dining room that neither of them ever spent any time in. On the medium-brown wood table that seated twelve people, he set their plates on crimson colored placemats that were trimmed in gold. The candles that set in the middle of the table were already lit. From the buffet on the wall at the far end of the dining room, Shane took the crystal top off of the stylish liquor bottle that he filled earlier in the day, to pour it into Cherie's Dublin-styled glass. He was more focused on getting his friendship on track than worrying about asking her if Terry had reached out to her lately. Every now and again, the thought would creep up on him that Terry was lurking in the shadows. To make it dissipate, he threw on a small smile and looked down at her, thinking of all the sacrifices that he made thus far just to be with her. Terry was no one, even though it kind of angered him to think that a man could finally get inside his head the way that Terry had.

Cherie smiled at him as she draped the gold napkin in her lap after sitting. As soon as he went to his placing, she sipped from the glass to find that it wasn't liquor that he poured.

"Pepsi." He smirked, lifting his glass.

She rolled her eyes at him and picked up her fork from beside her plate.

"Hope you don't mind," he told her, with his phone now in his hand. He mashed his screen a few times while sitting sideways in his chair. "The Boys are playing the Skins. I really don't want to miss this."

"Cowboys?" she asked with a full mouth.

With one last stroke against the gorilla glass face of his phone, the painting on the wall on the far end of the dining room lifted, and out came a 60-inch plasma.

"God, Shane," Cherie practically moaned with the tips of her first three fingers gently resting against her supple lips. "I underestimated you. This shrimp is to die for."

"Thanks, Rie." There was more air than words in his sentence. His eyes were on his plasma, closely watching his Redskins being pummeled by the oft-losing Cowboys.

Cherie hurriedly cut into her steak that was easy to slice through like butter. When she laid it on her tongue, she almost had an orgasm. Terry never cooked for her, and the only time Damon had, it was most likely stir-fry or pot roast. Shane threw down in the kitchen.

"C'mon!" he screamed, making Cherie flinch. He flailed his arms, slamming his back against the chair. "You see this shit? Cousins just threw away the fuckin' ball like Fat Boy Rob not even on the field!"

Daintily, Cherie picked up her napkin and dabbed the corners of her mouth with it. "Excuse me, dear, but are you referring to Kirk Cousins?"

"I know you see this clear ass nigga on my TV, Rie."

"I don't know why you're so mad. He's not even a real quarterback.

Now Romo? That's a real quarterback."

"Fuck you just say to me?"

"You heard me." She smirked.

"You want to take it there? You sure you want to go there with me, Rie?"

"I've already parked, got out, gave you the address to meet me, and now I'm staring you in the face, De'Shane. What's up?"

"I know she... I know she didn't."

"Did, done, and will do it again."

"You talkin' shit about my quarterback, bruh."

"You *won't* talk shit about *mine*."

"You a big girl now, huh?"

"Been a big girl about my Boys."

Shane stood out of his seat and popped his neck. Cherie had to be out of her damn mind to go against his team. What either of them hadn't noticed was that they were in the swing of things; just like how they were twelve years ago. They were only missing Mandy and Rich in the background to cheer them on or to step in when need be.

"Let me tell you somethin' about Romo. He only got twenty-nine yards last season and one touchdown pass. In his overall career, he got 34,183 yards. Don't play with a nigga that got 4,917 yards last season *alone* and twenty-five touchdown passes. In his entire NFL career, he got 12,113 yards. Romo ain't seein' him, even when the nigga got the flu."

"Uhh... but according to Google Alerts, Cousins *still* threw that ball away, and Romo *still* spankin' that ass on offense." She held up her cellphone to him to show him the stats about the game that was playing. "Where's all that mouth, De'Shane? Hmm? Don't play with me when you know I know all about football. Or did you forget that I'm pretty but will beat that ass in your backyard, boy?"

"Oh, you wanna go?" He slammed his fist inside the opposite hand with force.

Finally, Cherie stood out of her seat, planting her knuckles against the tabletop. "You couldn't handle me on the grass if you tried."

"Take the heels off then, girl. It's a backyard here, remember? We can do this."

Cherie's nostrils flared at the veins in Shane's arms. She wanted him to clear the table and take her within them. To be as rough with her as he looked to be at the moment. He could tackle her tight-end any day.

"Interception!" the announcer yelled, cutting the tension in the room.

Their heads snapped toward the plasma.

"Redskins' ball! Boy, I tell ya. Romo's night has taken a turn for the worst."

"That's what the fuck I'm talkin' about!" Shane roared. "Where's your mouth, Rie? Hmm?" He cupped his hand around his ear to get a listen for her comeback.

Surprisingly, she pecked him on the cheek and took her seat. "You better be glad that you can cook, and I don't want my food to get cold."

"Yea, okay. Let that be the excuse." Shane smirked as he sat.

"Don't talk shit. I can still take these six-inches off."

You'll be coming out of something else soon, he said to himself as he sipped his Pepsi.

Almost as if she could hear his thoughts, Cherie slipped her shoe off her foot and caressed his leg through his denim. As she forked her rice into her mouth, Shane narrowed his eyes at her while frozen in place. It was payback for when he had her on hush at the steakhouse when she had gotten back to Virginia.

"Really?" he asked her.

They hadn't been close since his potential wedding almost three months prior. Their lives with working, Miracle, and Cherie trying to conceive wouldn't allow them any time to be still or to be in the same room.

Cherie bit the corner of her bottom lip as she twirled her foot at the seat of his jeans. Beneath the ball of her small foot, she could feel him grow.

"You enjoyin' yourself?" he asked her.

"Maybe," she returned, pushing another forkful of her rice into her mouth.

"Okay. You're going to pay for that."

When, daddy? she asked in her head.

"You just wait patiently, Mon Cherie," he purred. Shane had a look in his eye that she knew all too well. He was going to catch her when she least expected it.

When they were younger and Cherie would hit him, he would lie in wait to get his lick back. He would only strike days or weeks later and would surprise the hell out of her with a painful sting to the back of her neck.

"You better not hit me," she remarked.

"Oh, I'm gonna hit you alright."

The two enjoyed the rest of the game, throwing insults here and there about each other's teams until they were almost stuffed. They ventured to the kitchen where they washed dishes together and finally retired for the night. Shane walked Cherie out to her car without pressuring her into staying for the night. He figured that she had enough of forceful Shane. She wanted her friend back, and that's exactly what he had given her. Things seemed much more smooth without all of the drama or the dark side of him rearing its ugly head.

Cherie felt how much lighter he was. It made her ride home with a smile on her face. After her shower and checking her schedule for the next day, she laid down with that beaming smile still on her lips. Finally, she closed her eyes, only for them to pop right back open at a text notification.

Lazily, she reached over and grabbed it, noticing that the friend she had regained sent her the message.

"You didn't tell me you were home, big headed ass girl." It read. *"Hope you really enjoyed yourself. Goodnight, Rie."*

"Oh, and by the way… Romo still sucks monkey balls. Now you can have a good night."

She stifled her smile as if he was somewhere in the room, all to reply to his message. *"Fuck you and the Redskins! Dak is king! And I didn't make it home!"*

"Well, then where you at?"

"I hit a unicorn in the road, and then aliens shot across the sky. They abducted me and told me to take them to my leader."

"Mmmhhmm… so where you at though?"

"I'm in DC. Duh! Where else would I be?"

"Whatever, lol. Goodnight, Rie."

"Night, lopsided head ass boy."

Cherie gave a schoolgirl-like sigh as she relaxed against her thick, king sized pillow. It felt good to live and breathe freely for a change. She had to let go of her fears of something waiting right around the corner to pop out and ruin them. It would be hard to do, but with more nights like this one, she was sure that it would make it much easier.

CHAPTER THREE

Babe

*W*ith a peaceful slumber that consisted of raunchy dreams, Cherie couldn't be more than happy. Shane's wet tongue was lapping her womanhood in her dream, and if anyone dared to call her phone or to burst through her bedroom door, they would most likely catch the beat-down of a lifetime. That was all until she realized how real the dream seemed.

Cherie found herself calling out his name in soft moans. In her dream, she reached for his dreadlocks to pull them, and even those felt a little too real. She was close to an orgasm when she decided to open her eyes and look down at the sheets. She snatched them off and found the real deal there, slurping on her pearl tongue.

"Shane?" she shrieked.

"Call me, baby," he grumbled against her in between smacks.

"Oh, God! What are you doing here?" It sounded more like she was whining. She hadn't known if it was the shock that pushed her away from her orgasm, or the excitement of him actually doing what she craved for.

"Cum for me, baby."

"No!" she cried. Cherie might've opposed, but she was loving the tongue she missed so much. Damon and Terry couldn't touch Shane's skills, even if they sat, watched, and took notes.

Shane slithered his wide hand up her stomach until he found her nipple. His warm and gentle touch made Cherie open her legs a little wider, as her hands pushed his head further into her pussy, damn near drowning the man in her wetness. As soon as Shane squeezed her sensitive flesh, Cherie's knees buckled. He knew that she was close.

Because of her little antic the night prior, he waited for her legs to vibrate and shake a little harder; then he stopped altogether and stood out of her bed.

"What the fuck?" she screeched. "What're you doing?"

"I told you that I would get you back, didn't I?" He wiped his mouth with the back of his hand.

"You evil sonofabitch!"

He winked at her with his infamous smirk gracing his face. "You have a good day now, Cherie."

"Shane!" she called as he walked out of her bedroom door casually. "De'Shane-motherfucking-Hartford! You get back here!"

"Love you!" he called over his shoulder.

"How do you even know where I live?" Angry, she slammed her back against her headboard and folded her arms. "Fucker," she mumbled.

If Cherie's day couldn't get any better, she sat on the stool inside of Royal Six's, waiting for Erykah to show, when she received a message that was a meme from Shane about Tony Romo. She rolled her eyes at it and reminded him of how racist the Redskins brand was.

"Now get off my quarterback before I have to come and see you," she threatened as she concluded her message.

"Come and see me," he replied. *"You got to find me first."*

"Morning!" Erykah cheered as she entered the boutique. She pulled off her shades and handed Cherie a cup of Starbucks coffee. "Excited about being back?"

"Something like that! What's this?" she asked happily as she eagerly took the coffee from Erykah's hand.

"I want you to come to a convention with me a few months away from now. I want to give you my connects so you can start your own hustle."

Her head snapped behind her as Erykah happily swayed into her office to put her purse away. "You want me to open my own shop, Erykah?" she inquired curiously. "Are you trying to get rid of me?"

"No," Erykah assured her with a giggle as she returned. "I just know that you pull in major commission on your own. It wouldn't be right for you to just sit up under my thumb. Besides, I kicked a job offer to April."

"God." Cherie relaxed her neck, dropping her head backwards. "Did you see her side of the church? It was so empty that I wanted to snatch weave of what little women did show up for her."

"Right. You should've been at the bachelorette party. If that's what you want to call it."

"What happened?"

"Alyssa had to put her foot up April's sister's ass. She was so disrespectful that it made me want to smack the shit out of her. But nooo, Quita just had to keep nudging me, telling me to let April stand up for herself. And then, the saddest part of the night was her confessing to some shit that happened to her when she was a kid. This Nicola bitch blamed her for being molested by their dad and for having their lives altered."

"That's stupid."

"Exactly. Rie, I'm telling you that you would've wanted to hop across the table on old girl."

"I feel really bad, you know. She almost married a great man, but her mind wasn't on it. It was on trying to get me and Shane back together. I stole her wedding, Erykah. She handed me a man that would've been so good for her."

"No, he wouldn't have been. He would've been living a damn lie, and she knew so. Just like the rest of us. Don't blame yourself for that. April knew what she was doing. Hell, I almost passed out before she raised her hand because I was holding my breath and staring directly at your ass."

"Me and Shane were that obvious?"

"As clear as freshly cleaned windows."

"Hey, do you have her number? I want to talk to her about something. I know a friend who's in the same place that she is right now. You remember the chick I was telling you that fucked my ex while I was still in the house?"

"Yea." Erykah fondly nodded, knowing exactly where Cherie was going with this.

"I was browsing through Instagram the other day and I saw that he was still single. He has money, he's handsome, he's funny, and he's such a gentleman. At first, I thought that he was beating Roxanna, but he wasn't. Turns out she was cheating and that's where her bruises came from. I heard that from another one of our friends. Anywho, I can invite him down one day and have them link up."

"Good deal. I'll let April know that you're sending someone her way. You hit up old boy and let him know that he has someone coming to him that's way better than this Roxanna bitch."

"I'll DM him."

Erykah sipped her coffee when a thought hit her. "Did you tell Shane about you trying to have a baby?"

Cherie eyed her closely, trying to figure out how she knew.

"Mama told me. She's nervous for you. You're going to have to tell Shane, Rie. You wind up pregnant, he might disconnect again."

"I know." She frowned.

"In the meantime, you got your notes from the e-mails? We need to get on crafting. I'm going to let you design today so you can get used to it. If you can do it yourself, it cuts down on the cost of having someone to do it for you."

"Honey, I need all the funds I can get."

The day went smoothly, all until Erykah and Cherie were knee-deep in molting silver when someone tapped on the bell that sat on the front counter for service. Cherie pulled off her industrial gloves and her apron to tend the customer. To her surprise, it was a delivery service from a company called Sprinkles. She frowned at them before slapping a smile on her face.

"How may I help you?" she politely asked the man who held a large pink box in his hands.

"Yes, ma'am. You have a special delivery. You have a great day." Before Cherie could thank him, the man whisked out of the door.

"What is it?" Erykah asked over her shoulder.

Cherie pulled the card from between the tightly wrapped bow, then opened it to read it aloud. "For the two hardest working women that I know. Enjoy. What you don't eat, give to the customers. Don't get greedy, now. Signed, Shane."

"He's such an ass when he's trying to be sweet," Erykah commented.

"But isn't he so sweet?" Cherie gushed. "I love Sprinkles!"

"I'm pretty sure he knows that."

"Hey, Erykah… what's your brother's favorite food?"

"What?" Her face twisted. "You mean to tell me that you don't know that maniac's favorite food? *The* Shane? Your everything?"

"Shamefully, no."

"Girl, it's simple. Shane will eat anything green, except cucumber.

He's mildly allergic. Red meat of any kind and it has to be well-done. My brother has a god-complex, so you might want to keep that in mind. He cherishes the temple that is his body. If it ain't clean, he ain't eatin' it."

"Got it."

"Slim options for seafood. Only salmon and shrimp. He doesn't like sushi. Nothing with mushrooms. His favorite meal is roasted chicken breast on quinoa with white cheddar over that. Open up an Angry Orchard or pour up some Brandy and Coke with that, he'll be putty in your hands."

"And dessert?"

"There is only one. See, this is classified information. Don't tell him that I told you." Erykah moved a little closer to Cherie then. "You want to see Shane go ape-shit over anything in his life… put a piece of cheesecake in front of him and then snatch it back."

"He loves it that much?"

"He's a health nut. He doesn't really eat sweets. He slashes throats over that cheesecake."

"I see." Cherie tapped her pointer finger on her chin. "Hey, Erykah, do you think you can watch Miracle Friday night?"

"Of course, but what you got up your sleeve?"

"Since Shane likes surprises, I'll give him a surprise."

———

Shane had met with April over lunch to give his apologies. It had been three months since they almost wed, so he thought that if there were any wounds, they would be close to healing by now. April gave him a friendly hug before parting ways with him, reminding him not to be a stranger. To show that he wouldn't be, he sent her a text when he had gotten inside his Hummer.

Then, he had gone to Rich's to relax for a little bit. Working wasn't as easy as Shane had thought it would be with the way he would forget or could've sworn that he had already done something. It was irritating at times, but mercifully he had Rich and Alyssa to back him.

When he walked through the front door, the first thing that he smelled was the sweet perfume of a woman. He gathered that Alyssa was there or had just left. Since his surgery, some of his senses were at an all-time high. He could hear and smell what others rarely could.

"What it is, bruh?" Rich said with a grin as he jogged down the steps of his home.

Shane exchanged their signature handshake when Rich reached the bottom of the steps. "Ain't shit with it. Got a text from Erykah saying that she was going to pick up Miracle, so I got about an hour to burn before I go home and get some sleep."

"How are the headaches?"

"Ain't been none in a minute."

"You still can't drink yet?"

"Not at all," he chuckled. "Just in case I'm going to have to take my pain meds."

Rich slapped his arm, then escorted Shane to the living room. "I talked to Mandy," he told him as he dropped down into his recliner.

"Word?" Shane pulled up the legs of his jeans to sit on the plush sofa. "What happened?"

"It's been damn near a year, but she's still pissed off. I figured that she would be over it by now, but she ain't. She still doesn't see what she did to make me leave her. That's a deep ass problem that females have. How can you not see when you have temper-tantrums for nothing?"

"Cherie gets stuck in her ways, but I'll give her medicine to calm that shit down."

"Yea, but every woman is different. You can't give 'em sex for medicine and think everything will be cool again. It's like I told Amanda. It had gotten to the point where I was disgusted at the sight of her. When she was naked in front of me, it was a turn-off. I can't fuck you, and you just got done callin' me every dog ass name in the book, fam."

"I hear you."

"She slapped the shit out of me before I left the restaurant, though. She told me that she hoped me and Lyssa had a baby with special problems. Then she turned around and said that she hopes I get Lyssa pregnant and we have a stillborn."

"Shit," Shane chorused. He leaned forward to get a better look at his friend. "She was that mad?"

"*That* mad, bruh."

"Them some hateful ass words."

"You tellin' me! You're wishing hate on my unborn?"

"Lyssa pregnant?"

39

"Hell naw. Birth control and condoms. She ain't ready for kids."

"Let me ask you a question." Shane massaged his goatee for a second before he could get his question out. He didn't know if he really wanted the answer to it. "What do you see in Lyssa that you didn't see in Mandy?"

"You sure you want to know the answer to that?"

"Hell yea, I want to know."

Rich took a deep breath and slid to the edge of his seat. "For real? Lyssa don't throw no damn tantrum with you. She might give you a look if she doesn't trust some shit, but she ain't gonna ride your back about it. Lyssa don't complain about a damn thing. She works her ass off and likes to handle things herself. You catch her pokin' her lips out, and it's only because she's hungry and don't know what the hell she wants to eat. It ain't a battle with my baby. Either we take it on together, or one of us dominate the fuck out of the problem to get it resolved. Lyssa is on a whole other level. Just because Mandy was my childhood sweetheart, it doesn't mean that I had to take her shit. Why you think I had to hook you up with April? Nigga, I was trying to give you options and to show you that you didn't have to be tied down. In your case, though, you can't help who and what you want. The ties are too strong. Them ties were loose than a motherfucker with me and Mandy, even though I tried."

"I understand. Trust me, I do."

"I want to talk to you about something, too."

"What's that?"

"Now, I know that Apollo ain't here no more, and you're my boy, so I really have to run this by you?"

"You want your own hustle?"

"Ain't got shit to do with business, bruh." Rich got up to leave the room, leaving Shane wondering what he could've been talking about. When he returned, he handed Shane a velvet box over his shoulder.

Shane took it and opened it. The ring inside made him push his fist up to his mouth in awe. The fourteen-karat white gold band was exquisite. The three stones that sat atop it were even more breathtaking, but what Shane loved the most was that the large diamond in the middle was canary yellow. He estimated the stone to be about 2.5 karats, costing at almost $5,000.

"This motherfucker is handcrafted," Shane marveled as he inspected it. "This diamond is laser-cut, and how they put the white diamonds in this bitch? Somebody had some seriously steady hands. They're perfectly symmetrical, Rich."

"Never lost your attention to detail, I see," Rich chuckled. "I'm glad you like it. Yellow is her favorite color."

"Are you… are you asking me for my blessing to marry my sister?"

"What you think?"

"That this is one hell of an expensive promise ring," Shane joked.

Rich playfully snatched the box out of his hand, snapping it shut in the process." So, what you say? Can I have Alyssa as my own? I promise to love and cherish her for as long as we both shall live."

"You know she's crazy, right?" Shane asked skeptically.

"I do," he chuckled. "But I love even that about her."

"Look, I told you before that it ain't me that you have to worry about if you fuck up with her. If you think that this is the move for you, and you trust it… go for it. Whatever you do… don't break her heart, bruh."

"Shit, you ain't got to tell me twice."

————

With work over, checking on Miracle and the rest of his family, Shane finally made it home. Before he pressed his thumb against the panel, he could smell the chicken and something like charcoal in the air. Odd, because he didn't remember putting any food on. Before he entered, he tried his best to remember if he had or hadn't. Finally settling on the fact that someone must've cooked for him, he entered his home and ventured into the kitchen.

On the island was a plate with roasted chicken breast sitting lovely atop a bed of quinoa. A card rested against the plate with pretty cursive writing on it. Cautiously he picked up to read it.

"Eat up. You'll need your strength. Xoxo, Rie."

With a smirk, Shane washed his hands in the kitchen sink, then pulled his cellphone from his back pocket after popping his plate into the microwave. He sent a text to Cherie, thanking her for the food she cooked for him. She sent back, "No problem. Enjoy."

Without knowing, he exposed the fact that he had finally made it home.

When he was done with his food, he traveled up to his room where he smelled lavender, hearing the slow drip of water inside of his jacuzzi tub. He entered, witnessing the steam rise from the purple colored water. He had to smile at it. It seemed as though he wasn't the only one who liked to surprise others.

Shane took his time to soak in the tub. Feeling completely relaxed, he sent Cherie a message that told her that she knew how to get him to calm down and sink into bliss. After a while, he finally let the water out of the tub and dried himself off. Then, he went into his room where he stopped dead in his tracks.

"First down," Cherie said with a sexy smirk. She was dressed in nothing but a white Dak Prescott jersey, sitting on her knees with her hands firmly pressed into the mattress. "Got somethin' you want to do to me, Redskin?"

Without a breath, in his lungs, since Cherie took it away, he dropped his towel and slowly approached the bed.

Cherie stood and walked on the tips of her toes toward the foot of it to grab onto the iron bar that suspended the parted sheer drapes. Shane circled his bed with flexing nostrils. He was reminiscent of a wild beast, stalking his prey. No matter how far they drifted apart, Cherie would always warm his blood.

Her thick, oiled thighs were his kryptonite. His jaws gathered plenty of saliva just by looking at them or from having them in his peripheral. To tease him a little more, she lifted one of her legs and laid it over his shoulder. With one of her hands, she set his dreads free from the bun they were in so that they could fall how she liked them.

"I'm not cheesecake," she said in a sultry voice, "but I have something else for you to eat for dessert."

Shane's reply was to tilt his head back and kiss her unmentionable lips underneath her jersey. He didn't know which part excited him more. If it was the fact that she pulled a him on him, or if it was because he thirsted for her so long and was finally able to drink her rivers down.

"Fuck, Mon Cherie," he said in a thick, French accent.

That alone almost drove her to that orgasm that he teased her with a few days ago. Maybe she would be sneaky and try to steal his man juice for her baby.

CHAPTER FOUR

Mother, May I?

Days of Cherie and Shane poking fun at each other, watching football together, and looking after Miracle were days that Cherie could only wish for. She received them and truly enjoyed the bliss. Most times she would become saddened when thinking that they could've had it a while ago, but they both had to grow and go through tests, trials, and come into their own before they could get to this point. There was still no mention of Terry or the baby to either of them. Their happy place was more important at the moment.

Today, however, they were sitting in an examination room after Shane received a CT scan to make sure that everything with his brain was functioning normally. It was officially a year since he had his surgeries, and he still didn't feel like himself.

Cherie squeezed his hand while they waited for the doctor to enter. She lent him a little of her strength; just like how she used to when they were children. She wasn't sure if it was working, but she hoped for the best.

"Good evening!" Dr. Lowe swayed into the room with Shane's

chart in his hand. His piercing blue eyes landed on Cherie, and his smile was to die for. "How are we, mademoiselle?" Gently, he reached for Cherie's hand and kissed it when she offered it to him.

"Worried about my De'Shane," she giggled. "How's he looking, doctor?"

"Mr. Hartford!" Dr. Lowe gave Shane a manly handshake before he took his seat on a small stool near the couple. "You are healing very well. There's no damage or infection to or in the tissues of your scar. Your wavelengths seem to be functioning normally, and your responses are on point."

"What about short-term memory?" Shane asked, almost forgetting that Cherie was sitting right next to him. She was his best friend, after all, so she could hear whatever the matter was. The only thing that would concern him about anything was that she would worry. He hated it when she was a worry-wart.

"That'll get better with time, of course. I recommend fish oils and brain-teasers. Have there been any nosebleeds?"

When Shane didn't answer, Cherie leaned away from him and stared at the side of his face.

Shane cleared his throat. "Actually, a few weeks ago, there was only one."

Cherie clenched her jaw. He hadn't told her of it happening.

"It didn't last long though. After I cleaned my nose and blew into the tissue, that was it. It hadn't happened before or after that."

"Were you stressing over anything at the time?" Dr. Lowe asked as he jotted down notes within Shane's file.

"I had just got done doing a couple of reps. It was arms day at the gym."

"Your temperature must've risen at almost 102 degrees. That's normal. You might want to be mindful of things like that. You can't overwork, over think or stress."

Cherie didn't let Shane get away with that. She waited for him to go over his speech therapy so that Dr. Lowe could make sure that he wasn't falling behind with it. Then, he gave Shane a few reflex tests to ensure that his motor skills were deadlocked. After everything checked out, Cherie waited for Shane to sit her in the car and for him to get in before she ranted.

"You couldn't tell me about your nosebleed, why?" she complained.

"It was once, and it wasn't a big deal." Shane started the car and pulled away from his space.

"Yea, and I've been on fertility treatments, but that's not a big deal either, is it?"

Shane mashed his brakes. He didn't think that he heard her correctly. "What did you say to me?"

"I've been trying to get pregnant, but I haven't told you! Is it a big deal?"

"I got to be honest and say that I don't even come close to seeing the damn correlation."

"We haven't been talking to each other about what's important, Shane. We've just been having fun."

"You're mad at me because I didn't tell you about a two-second nosebleed, but you didn't think that it was important for me to know about you trying to have a baby? A whole one? Cherie, what the hell? That makes no sense. Yea, I get it, I should've told you... maybe. But if we're rekindling our friendship and shit, don't you think I should've known about a baby? That's on a whole different level."

"I didn't know how to tell you." She took her attention to the side of his face. Cherie was lucky that he hadn't been staring at her. If he had, she wouldn't have been able to get her words together. "I guess I was just mad at you for keeping something from me, yet I was keeping something, too. I'm sorry."

"Cherie, you could've told me anything. You know I love you, girl. That ain't an excuse."

"I know but—"

"I really don't want to be a hypocrite right now and say that I'm kind of jealous that you're trying to have a baby without me because I have Miracle. But... it's the way I feel right now. I mean, I know that I always thought that me and you would do so much and go so far... but that shit stings."

"How do you think I feel about you and Jessica? It gets worse because she's my sister, dearly departed. Shane, if we continue, my niece is going to be my step-daughter."

"I know that, but that's way off subject right now. A baby is more than a little nosebleed. You and I weren't on talking terms when I found out about my daughter. We're cool as fuck now, so you could've told me."

"And about me and Jessica being sisters?"

"I honestly don't know how to feel about it, so I don't really have anything to say about it. I loved two sisters once upon a time." He shrugged. "That's not my focus right now. My focus is on you doin' whatever you have to do to get a baby. I'm wondering how come you didn't even think to ask me to be a donor, if need be. You out here fuckin' for a baby, Rie?"

"Can we not do this?"

"You do that when you're scared of something. You purposely avoid everything or want to drop it when you're wrong."

"Shane—"

"Are you fuckin' to get a baby?" His tone rose, and all it did for Cherie was make her keep her mouth closed. He was back to frightening her. Even worse, she couldn't tell him that when they weren't speaking, when he was about to marry April, she hooked up with Damon a few times. "Answer me."

Cherie gulped instead of responding.

Shane decided to keep quiet. He pulled out of the parking lot and took her to her condo. Just when things were looking up, they slid downhill again. This time, it was nowhere near his fault.

———

After dropping Cherie off, Shane had gone to the Big House to retrieve his blessing from Mama J. What he walked upon was Miracle jetting out of the sitting room and into the dining area. She ran past

Stuck On You 2

him so quickly that it made him flinch.

"Miracle Serenity Hartford! Get back here!" Mama J yelled. She stumbled past the couch and jogged across the foyer to find her granddaughter somewhere in the dining room. "You let that go," Shane heard Joyce complain. "Open your mouth! You spit that out! Give it to GG. Miracle, open your mouth."

Shane shook his head as he made his way into the dining area to see Joyce standing behind his daughter, leaning over her so that she could dig into the toddler's mouth.

"Ren, what you got?" he asked calmly with a smile.

On cue, she released her jaws so that Joyce could get out the small piece of plastic that Miracle somehow confiscated from the trashcan.

"Finally." Joyce huffed as she inspected it.

Shane picked his daughter up and propped her on his forearm. "You givin' GG a hard time, Ren?" he asked her.

"You wouldn't believe. She's nowhere near two years old, yet, and she's already bad as hell. All that energy is going to give her granny a stroke."

"You're not that old, Ma," Shane chuckled as he lightly bounced his prize.

Joyce had her thick curls in three ponytails with balls around them. She had two up top and one in the back. Miracle was already dressed, ready for her father to come and retrieve her. Joyce dressed her in a dress that had a white, two-layer ruffle skirt and an attached navy blue and white striped tank top.

Shane tugged at the chiffon bow on the chest of Miracle's top to tease her. "Why are you givin' GG a hard time, Ren? I thought I told you to be a good girl this morning."

"Just because you tell her, doesn't mean she's going to do it, De'Shane."

"I know," he chuckled.

"How was your check-up?" Joyce pulled out her favorite chair at the head of the long table and took a seat with her eyes still on her son.

"It was alright. I told him about a nosebleed I had, but he didn't think it was major. My body is back to normal, but my thoughts and my mind are not."

"What does that mean?"

"I have short-term memory loss like hell, Ma. I mean, it's not as bad as it was a few months ago, and it's getting better. It's just worrisome, you know. My motor skills are at one-hundred-percent. Vision is twenty-twenty. Verbal skills are back to normal. It's just the memory that's holding me back."

"Like you said, it'll get better. You had a major surgery, Shane. Your memory was horrible when the girls were helping you out. They told me that you would be in the middle of a sentence and get angry because you forgot what you were about to say, or forgot what you were doing in the middle of actually doing it. You've come so far. It's going to get better. You're still healing."

Shane kissed Miracle's cheek. She was busy tugging and running her fingers through her father's trimmed and short chin hair.

"What's on your mind?"

Shane looked over at her, trying to figure out if he should put his infamous invisible mask on for her or not. "Just… life," he honestly spoke. "Cherie's trying to have a baby, and we're trying to get back to our happy place. She just told me about it, even though it didn't have nothin' to do with our conversation."

"Are you upset about it?"

"Kind of. Having Miracle in the middle of so much hurt made me happy, ma. Just being with my daughter makes everything better for me. I think Cherie deserves this kind of happiness."

"Oooh, she doesn't deserve Miracle's happiness! Your daughter has gotten bad! And she's stubborn as hell! GG loves her Renny-Ren, but Lord! Take her home with you! Get out! Go!"

"You know, Ren… if your Pop-Pop was still livin', he would've dusted off your backside for running through his sitting room like that."

"No, he wouldn't, baby," Joyce told Miracle. "GG would've tightened his leash if he ever raised his hand to you."

Miracle readjusted herself and rubbed her face inside the chest of Shane's white polo.

"It's nap time," Shane said with a chuckle. "I'll get her home, Ma. She's the only woman that will ever make me truly hop-to."

"Congratulations, son. You are a slave for this little woman for the rest of your life."

"Tell me about it."

Two hours of being home, and Shane fed his daughter, changed her clothes, her diaper, and set her in front of the TV inside her playpen. Hanging halfway off the couch, he ended up dozing off. The only thing to wake him was the sound of his ringing phone. His eyes fluttered open to it scrolling across the coffee table. He cleared his throat, sat up, and grabbed his screaming device.

"What's up?" he answered.

"Headed to take care of some business," Bo told him. "I'll be out of town for a while. You need somethin'?"

"No," Shane replied groggily as he wiped the sleep from his eyes. "Just make sure nobody talks you out of six million."

"Come on now. You know I'm a veteran. Ain't nobody talkin' me out of nothin'."

"You talked to Rich?"

"I did. And let me tell you somethin'. You need to keep an eye on him. Apollo was my boss before he was my best friend, so it was different. He was your best friend before you became his boss. People change, Shane. Lastly, I don't like to have a motherfucker keepin' tabs on me. I was doin' this shit before that boy was even thought about. You hear me? I ain't ever had to check in with anybody, let alone a young one who only thinks he's runnin' shit. You handle that before you end up plannin' his funeral."

Bo hung up, leaving Shane to look at the screen of his phone. What the hell did he mean by "checking in"? He had never told Bo to check in with anybody. Bo should've never gone along with it in the first place.

Miracle took his attention away from growing angry with a bang of her plastic rotary dial phone. He looked over at the playpen. Instantly, a smile grew onto his face.

"Ren, what you doin'?"

She looked back at her father with her pacifier in her mouth. The look on her face told Shane that he was interrupting her play time. With the way she reacted to her special nickname, Shane thought that she grow to ignore him when he called her, simply because he cut her middle name— Serenity— short to just Ren.

Shane rolled off the couch and belly-crawled over to the playpen. Then, he made funny faces at her just to make her laugh. Having the feeling that she had spent enough time caged up, he collapsed his side of her pen, having her quickly crawl over to him and grab both sides of his face.

"You can't have a kiss," he told her. "Where are your clothes, Ren? I know I put you on a t-shirt and socks before I dozed off."

Miracle smashed her pacifier into her father's lips anyhow for the kiss he wouldn't give, and even that brought a smile to his face.

Over her, Shane saw her strewn t-shirt and socks on the mat of her pen. He looked down into those gorgeous, dirty green eyes of hers and smirked. "You just like to be a naked baby." Roughly, he grabbed her as he turned over onto his back. His daughter's laughter made him forget about his day or things that he was going to have to handle soon. "You can't be a naked baby," he teased as he tossed her. "Naked babies get sick. No naked babies!"

Again, his phone rang, sliding close to the edge of the coffee table. The chorus of John Legend's "Love Me Now" blared throughout his living room. He knew that it was Cherie's ringtone, but he chose not to answer right off. Shane didn't want to say something that would hurt her feelings, or sit quietly on the phone without something nice to say. She surprised and hurt him today. Maybe she was calling to apologize or confess. Either way, he was with his leading lady, and her phone call would have to wait. How would he even look her in the face knowing that she was sleeping with someone to try and have a baby?

CHAPTER FIVE

The Edge Of The Unknown

*L*ost in desperation, Cherie jumped at the opportunity to go to Alyssa's birthday dinner. She was surprised that nobody said anything about Shane's since it was strongly approaching. For three days, he hadn't spoken to her. If she knew him like she thought she did, then she would know that he was only getting his head together. The urge of cursing him out and reprimanding him for ignoring her was at the edge of her brain. She started to go to dinner just to hem him up in a corner somewhere, but she didn't need to be the old her. They were trying to bring back the fires of their passion, and that would be one way to fan them off.

She checked herself in the mirror atop her dresser as she smoothed her hands over her hips. Her pencil skirt was fitting nicely, and so was her strapless blouse. Purposely, she had gone a day prior to get a tattoo. It was an infinity symbol just above her armpit. It was classy and easy to cover if she ever chose to work in an office.

Her phone lit up in the mirror, and even when shown backward, she readily recognized a number that she didn't want to see.

She yanked it up and placed it on speaker. "What, Roxanna?"

"I don't mean to bother you," Roxanna spoke meekly. "Terry has been missing for a week. Has he gotten in contact with you?"

"Why the hell would he be contacting me in the first place? Didn't you say that he wished death on me or some shit like that?"

"Well, yea, but—"

"And didn't I tell you that he was your problem and not mine?"

"Cherie, you don't understand! I went through his bank statements to see that he pulled out a large sum of money!"

"Maybe he's running away from you? Ever thought of that?"

"He doesn't have a reason to. I'm trying to help you!"

"I don't need help from a woman who fucked a man who I was still technically engaged to while I was still in the same damn house." Angrily, Cherie hung up and smashed her phone against the dresser. She would later regret it, but for now, she had to straighten her tight, black curls that she had cut in layers. Her short cut did the length of her neck and her figure a justice. She shouldn't have been worried about it. She should've been worried about if or when Terry would pop up on her. Cherie had almost forgotten that he and Shane were on the same wavelength.

———————

When Cherie arrived at the restaurant that Apollo owned, a few of the sisters were dabbing away tears, while Shane and Rich were standing by the bar, toasting to something.

"What's with the water works?" she asked when she was close

enough to the table.

Joyce pulled out the chair next to her so that Cherie could be seated. "Rich proposed to Alyssa."

In mid-sit, Cherie's head leaned over to the side. Confusion was written all over her face. She had no idea that Rich left her own cousin for her potential sister-in-law. "Congratulations," she said anyway. "Did someone record it?"

"I did." Joyce handed Cherie her phone so that she could see the whole speech.

Because she couldn't hear the audio, she sent the message to her email. "I'll have to watch later. The chatter in here is too much right now." She handed Joyce her phone back, then reached across the table for Alyssa's hand. "Let me see the ring, Lyssa!"

Alyssa obliged and curved her wrist to let Cherie get a good look.

Cherie was floored. "Good Lord Almighty," she said breathlessly. "Will you look at that yellow diamond? That is gorgeous."

"It is." Alyssa sniffled. "It came out of the blue, girl. When you see the video, you're going to cry. Even Erykah gasped and shed a few tears."

Cherie let go of Alyssa's hand and flexed her fingers so that Erykah would know to hand King over. "He's so handsome in his little bowtie!" she gushed. "Look at you, King! I could just eat you up!"

"Don't eat my son," Erykah teased as she handed over her well-dressed son, in his denim bottoms, white and blue plaid button-up, and bowtie. Erykah put little Polo boots on his feet to tie his outfit together. "You tell Cherie that your uncle insisted on choosing your outfit for today."

"Girl, Shane's ass dressed everybody," Quita honed in.

That's when Cherie noticed the two different shades of blue— half the family wore navy while the other wore sky-blue— and white. She was the only person out of the dress code that she hadn't known about. She wore black and pearl. Cherie felt like Shane did it on purpose. Rich and Alyssa were the only ones who coordinated yellow into the mix. He must've known that Rich was going to propose.

In Joyce's lap sat Miracle, banging on the table. Her two-layer skirt was navy blue, while her short sleeve top was white along with her baby doll shoes. Shane had placed yellow barrettes in her hair, in front of her two curly ponytails, just to match her bracelet and her tiny string of pearls. Even King's bowtie was yellow. She wondered if the children would be taking some sort of pictures with Rich and Alyssa because they were well-coordinated.

"Rie, what's wrong?" Ashington asked over the table. "You look like you just turned green. You want a drink?"

"I'll get one," she returned. "Just not right now."

"Still got baby fever?"

"Ash, shut up," Alyssa said from beside her. "You can start a conversation without asking somebody something so personal."

"I'm just asking because of the way that she's looking at Miracle and King."

"Okay, but you don't *have* to ask."

"She's okay," Cherie spoke up. "They're just so gorgeous this evening."

"When are you going to have some little ones?" Ash asked.

Alyssa bowed her in the side. "Seriously, girl? Shut up!"

Out of nowhere, Miracle was being lifted into the air, and it made Cherie look up and over at Miracle's smile when she realized that her own dad had come to retrieve her from her grandmother's lap. Cherie felt that sting of anger and jealousy all over again. This time, she swallowed it. The father-daughter pair looked so happy together.

"The food's coming out in a little bit y'all," Rich announced as he took a seat across from Alyssa, right beside Cherie.

There was so much she wanted to say to him, but she chose to keep it to herself. She had already ruined one wedding. She wasn't going to ruin another.

After the food had arrived, all you could hear from the Cruz's table was laughter and chatter over the clinking forks against the china. King and Miracle weren't being passed from lap to lap. They were in their high-chairs, being fed by their parents.

"What's it like, Shane?" Rich asked suddenly. "I really want to know. To be a working, single father. What's it like?"

"The same as how it feels to be a working, single mother," he chuckled, raising his glass at Erykah.

She squished her lips together, almost as if to be blowing a kiss at her brother. She raised her glass, as well, and drank to the success of raising children by themselves.

"I mean, you have your good days and your bad days," Shane went on. "One sneeze from your kid, as a first-time parent, and you'll find yourself in someone's emergency room. It's like all time stops and you're running around the house with a Lysol can to get rid of germs. You're paranoid. But then you have your good days." Shane seemed to zone out as everyone listened intently to what he was saying. The tips of his pointer and third finger slowly caressed the rim of his brandy glass. "You have these days when you feel like everybody and everything is against you... When all the world seems like it's just on fire, and you're right in the middle of it all... When these clouds come over you and it dampens your mood... But then... you go home and see these big, glassy eyes staring up at you. They don't know what's going on or why you seem to be half-dead. They don't know that bills are due or that you're damn near breaking yourself in half to invest in their future and to keep a roof over their heads, clothes on their backs, and food in their bellies."

"How... how is that a good thing?" Rich inquired.

"Because one look into those eyes, my friend... makes the impossible, *possible*. One glance into those innocent orbs seems to make all that bad shit during your workday look like lollipops and rainbows. Your kids will give you some kind of second wind to go back to war the very next day, with your sword in the air and your shield at your side. They make it seem like you weren't wounded in the first place."

"Amen!" Erykah commented. "You better preach, brother!"

"Just coming home to them… disintegrates everything else."

"Bull." Rich laughed.

"None at all. Everybody at this table knew that I had some serious issues about losing, depression, and mental instabilities. But Miracle is my serenity. She's my greatest creation and the answer to all of my prayers. She makes me happy like no one else could, and she can't even talk yet. See, Rich… your kids will give you this unconditional love that you never thought was possible. She may grow up to date a jerk that I'm probably going to have to pistol-whip one day, but I will only back off for her. That's only if she tells me to. And that's because I love her. You, one day, will experience the feeling of loving someone you never knew. When that day comes, just look over at me, and I'll say, 'I told you so.'"

"Brother, you hit it right on the head," Erykah told him. "Even though King is crawling now, I still have to get after him. It angers me when he hides in the cabinets because I always think that someone has come in and stole my baby. But when I find him, all that anger melts away, and I laugh and laugh until I'm rolling around on the floor with him. Being a single parent, for me, is happiness in a bundle that I don't have to split or share with anybody. Believe me when I say that I enjoy that shit." She lifted her glass again before taking a sip. "Single parents get a bad rep sometimes, but it's the trying times that people boast on the most. They don't ever share any of the good. We ain't gon' sit here and tell you that it'll be easy, but we're telling you what you're going to enjoy so that you don't run from it." Erykah's eyes cut to Cherie then.

"Honestly, I can't wait," Cherie spoke. "To have my own little one… God, the experience will be heavenly."

Everybody's eyes went wandering around the table, except for Erykah and Joyce. They were truly lost at her statement.

Ashington just had to take the floor. "I thought you and Shane were going to be together."

Unlike any other time, nobody nudged her or told her to keep quiet.

"I mean… am I literally the only person here who's lost? After that wedding fiasco, I thought that y'all would've made up, and we would be planning your wedding next. Did I just step into the Twilight Zone? How or why are you having a baby and not mentioning my brother?"

Shane cleared his throat as he lifted his glass up to his lips. "Cherie had *prior* engagements, love. All that *didn't* include me."

"He's right," Cherie defended herself. "I started taking fertility drugs months ago because it was something that I had to do for me. Are you bitter about it, Shane?"

"Alright now," Joyce said lowly. She could feel the tension on either side of her.

"Just like you had to do what was right for you when *you* had unprotected sex."

All forks dropped. The family didn't know whether to be angry at Cherie or cheer because of her point.

Shane set his glass on the table and locked his fingers behind his head. "You right, I did. It was a goodbye fuck, and something amazing came out of it. Is you done, or is you finished?"

"I said alright," Joyce repeated herself.

Cherie was far from done. The family got to witness the venom between Shane and Cherie firsthand. "One last fling, huh? When you were so about me? Yea, something amazing came out of it, but I didn't get the chance to have her. I didn't get the chance to have you either."

"Oh, you had plenty of chances," Shane corrected her. He flattened his palms against the table, leaning forward to get a good look at Cherie. "It's not my fault that you messed them up. The first time, I get it. But the second time? I gave you the best, and you couldn't even be honest with me. So who really deserves to be mad at this table?"

"I do. Because no matter how hard we try, we always end up at each other's throats."

"The only way we end up like that is when you run away or want to throw daggers from your tongue because you're wrong."

"*Wrong?*"

"Yea, I said it. Cherie hates to be wrong, so she goes the extra mile to try and make somebody else look bad. Well, let me tell you something. I don't care how my daughter was made, who gave birth to her or when she came into this world. She's *mine* to claim. Didn't matter if *you* had her not. And the next time you need leverage in an argument, I advise you to leave her out of it."

"Shane," Joyce lowly called him. She found his hand on the table with her own and gave it a gentle squeeze. She could tell that the beast that was him, that he tried to keep locked away, was about to rear its ugly head. "Come on now, calm down."

"He doesn't have to calm down," Cherie said with her eyes

strongly slicing through his. "The truth is that Shane will throw anything in my face to help him remind me of how and why I didn't come back."

"That ain't got nothin' to do with this conversation," he fired off.

"Yes, it does. That's what you're always mad at. You mad at me for saying something about Miracle, or at the fact that I didn't come back? Which one is it this time? I told you that I wanted a baby, but by no means is that an excuse for you to sit here and be pissy now. No matter how you feel, I'm going to do what's best for Cherie, baby."

Shane slowly shook his head. "You're self-righteous, spoiled, and entitled when you don't even deserve the universe I tried to give you. I wouldn't doubt that you would make a good mother, and I pray to God that your prayers for a kid have been answered. But, Cherie... you can't *run* from a baby when you want them to stop crying."

"Stop—" Joyce tried, but she was cut off by her rambling son.

"You can't sit in your head when you can't figure out what the hell is making said child upset."

"Shane!"

"And by God... the attention won't be on you anymore. It's going to always be about that kid that you want so desperately. That ain't Cherie. Cherie has to have a monument, a parade for fixing a fucking bottle. She has to have everybody to bow down and kiss her ass because she changed a fucking diaper."

Joyce whacked him across the cheek to get him to keep quiet. "I said stop it, dammit!"

"She knows that I'm telling the truth, Ma. That's why we can never work. Yet, I sit here looking like the bad guy, because it's what she wanted since she's wrong. And she always will be wrong. Everybody sitting at this table has gone through shit, Cherie. But you think the world owes you something because you went through hell as a kid. We all did, but we're still pushing, and we're damn sure not wanting a baby to try and bandage the wounds of our mothers and father. Like I said, you're *wrong*." Shane stood out of his seat while grabbing Miracle out of her high-chair.

"You bastard!" Cherie said with a hiss. She too rose as she banged her hand against the clothed table. "How dare you assume anything about me?"

"It ain't assumptions," he returned calmly. "You tend to forget very often that I know you better than anybody else walking this planet. That, too, is how I know that you would rather fuck a whole other dude than to come to me for it. You didn't need to say it. I already knew."

"Alright!" Joyce yelled. She was thankful that they were in the family dining area, instead of with the other patrons, or else the diners would've had a free dinner show. Joyce slammed her hands down onto the table and stood in her four-inch pumps. To give her courage, she grabbed on to Apollo's golden rosaries that seemed to give her strength on a daily. "Now this is enough! You're acting like children. Petty-fucking-children! I have gone with Cherie to her therapy session when on these hormones, every appointment to receive her treatments, and I thoroughly understand why it is and how it is that she's getting this baby. Does it matter, Shane? She wants a baby, and it wasn't her decision to come to you. Does it fucking matter?"

Shane was more baffled that Joyce was swearing. He couldn't give her a statement.

"Cherie, you were wrong to throw Miracle in your argument, because you're getting ready to conceive a child that's not his either. Neither of you are in the right. Now, for once, we are going to sit here and have a goddamn dinner like a family, without bullshit thrown into the mix. We're going to sit here, hold a conversation, eat, and have a good damn time. That's whether you two like it or not. Either of you walk out of that door and it's your asses. I promise you that. Lastly, Ashington, if I hear one more inappropriate comment or question, I'm going to reach across this table and pop you in the lips. You're an adult. You're not a little baby that can get away with saying whatever flies out of your ass at the moment. Grow your ass up. You have three seconds to do so. Shane and Cherie, sit your asses down, let go of all of that anger, and celebrate Alyssa's birthday and her accepting Richard's proposal. The both of you are such drama queens that you make everything about the both of you without even trying. This is proof of that. But today, ain't about you. Wait until this dinner is over to rip each other's throats out for all I give a fuck, but until then, you will sit here and celebrate. Do we have a deal?"

Both of them were still heated at one another, so they chose not to say a thing.

"Alright. Since we're still acting like children, give one another a hug and say I'm sorry."

Both of them looked at Joyce as if she had lost her marble in that moment.

"Okay. Rich, grab Miracle for me."

Rich hadn't known why he was retrieving his niece, but with the tension in the room, he did as he was told.

Joyce leaned down to the floor, brought her large purse up, and slammed it onto the tabletop. She rummaged through it for all of two second before pulling out a shiny, chrome nine millimeter.

Shane and Cherie both jumped back when they heard the snap of her loading her bullet into the chamber. The rest of the family hopped out of their seats and backed away in case she was really going to let bullets fly freely throughout the dining area.

Joyce placed both hands on her hips while eyeing the two grown children. "I said hug and say I'm sorry," she repeated seriously.

Quickly, the two came together in an embrace, leaving out their apologies.

"Nope. Act like you goddamn mean it. Without a rebuttal."

This time, they hugged and held it.

"I'm sorry," Shane said first. "I shouldn't have gone off like that."

"Me too," Cherie replied. "I didn't have no business bringing up Miracle in anything."

"Now kiss," Joyce ordered.

They looked at her with furrowed brows then.

"You heard what I said. Hell, that's probably what all this fuss is about. Y'all ain't been hittin' the sheets regularly."

"Mama," Shane whined. "Come on now. We don't want to hear you talk like that. It's bad enough that you're cursing."

"I said *kiss*!"

Without any further questions, Shane grabbed Cherie's chin and smashed his lips onto hers. That spark that neither of them felt in a while sizzled until it was a full blaze. They couldn't explain where it had come from, but they were just happy to be out of that bad head space and into a better one, even though they were forced to do so.

"Now ain't that better?" Joyce asked them. "Damn, got to use my unladylike words and pull out guns just to make y'all act right. And the next time you're not seeing eye-to-eye, y'all need to talk to each other. Not throw flames at each other."

"But, he—" Cherie started.

"I don't give a damn if he wasn't answering your phone calls. Girl, you are a woman. Use your womanliness. That means go and knock on the goddamn door. He ain't home, report his car stolen. That'll get his damn attention."

"Hold on, Mama J," Rich interrupted her. "Now, that's taking things a little too far. Don't be givin' them no ideas like that."

"It ain't an idea. Y'all men are stubborn as hell, and sometimes you need to be put in your place. Sometimes, we got to get your attention because you're easily distracted."

"Ma, don't talk about men like that when we're standing right in front of you."

"Yea? Who's going to stop me?"

"I ain't stoppin' shit since you got that gun in your hand." Rich sat in his seat, with his niece in his lap. "As soon as you put it away, I don't have a problem telling you how you insulted me, or what women have a problem with?"

"Nuh uh." Alyssa went back to the table and pulled her chair out. "Mama, put the gun up. Let's talk about this. And what exactly do women have a problem with?"

Rich looked back at Shane for reassurance, like old times.

"Hell naw," he chuckled. "They outnumber us, bruh. You're on your own with this one."

Cherie leaned over and whispered to Shane, "I need to talk to you about something really important. I'll meet you back at your house. But... we have to talk like adults. I hate going at it with you."

Shane lightly nodded. His stomach churned at the thought of them having to have a mature discussion. To him, she was going to say some things that were most likely going to upset him. If he wanted to continue to be with her, he was going to have to do it.

CHAPTER SIX

Anything Could Happen

Damon was in the middle of washing his dishes when he heard a faint knock on his front door. He hurriedly wiped his hands off on his dishtowel, then scurried to fetch the caller who decided to drop by. To his surprise, it was Cherie. She stood there, looking ever so beautiful in the outfit of her choosing for the night.

"You don't look pregnant," he said with a scowl. "What? You want to give it another try? I thought that you said we couldn't contact each other after that night."

"That's exactly what I said, Damon," she replied, lifting her head high. "I just want to say that, obviously, I'm not pregnant. I thank you for your assistance in helping me. Lastly, I'm sorry for seemingly using you."

"You can save your apology, alright? I knew what it was when you came to me. I just wanted to fuck one more time before you left."

"Excuse me?"

"You heard me. You were never with me. You used me as a

distraction from this dude. I know you did. It is what it is. Now you can go and be with him and make as many babies as you want."

"You know, Damon, I came over here trying to be an adult, but I can see that you're still scorned as fuck. I'll leave you to it."

"Scorned? No, baby. You're cursed. You can't ever move forward because you love a man who obviously doesn't love you back. You're stupid."

"And that's my cue to go because the name calling isn't called for."

"Yes, it is when I gave you love. Real love."

"Yea, okay. Take care of yourself."

Damon slammed the door so that he wouldn't see Cherie walk away from him.

She stood there with a smirk before she had the gall to walk right into his condo. She found him in the kitchen and slapped the taste out of his mouth for his disrespect. "The next time you get a good woman, you should focus on what you're doing instead of the man who holds her heart. Fuckin' steal it next time, pussy."

With pride, she left with a switch in her hips. She and Damon could've had a good thing, yet he was so wrapped up in her and Shane's madness that he lost his footing.

———————

Unfortunately, when Cherie arrived at the house that was made for her, Shane answered the door with lowered lids and a lazy smirk on his face. She shut her eyes tight, knowing already that he had too much to drink after she left.

SUNNY GIOVANNI

"Come on," she said as she entered, throwing his arm over her shoulder. She was going to have to help him to the bed because he was a little too tipsy to even stand straight up on his own.

Cherie stumbled when she had the chance to finally throw Shane onto the bed. Coincidentally, she landed on top of him. The two held a strong connection, locking eyes on one another. Even through his drunken haze, that spark between him and Cherie was there, and he could feel it.

"Why you even come?" he asked her. His breath reeked of liquor and all but he had to make his point to her. "Whatever you got to say to me shouldn't be about how you want out. You always want out for some reason."

"Shane, shut the fuck up." She rolled her eyes and tried to get up. The only thing to hold her down was Shane's wide hand on her lower back. She had to admit that she still liked his forcefulness. At the moment, he annoyed her, however.

"Was I that bad to you in the past?" he lowly asked her. "Did you really forget all of what we've been through, just to run out to California to be with that other nigga when I could've helped you clear your name?"

"I told you that *I* had to clear my name myself. Terry got me into some serious shit that I didn't want to be a part of. I would've been sent to federal prison, had I not done it."

"Yea, well it burned, Cherie."

"Shane, you're drunk. Sleep it off."

Again, he pulled her when she tried to leave. Their chests

smashed. Cherie lost her breath.

"I can't sleep off the fact that I've literally loved multiple women at the same damn time. The only constant was you. I don't know why we can't get it right. Maybe because I was so horrible to you. So forceful. Maybe because I didn't stop to ask you what you really wanted. Whatever it was—"

"It was me," she confessed. "I was always scared of what could've been. Afraid of ruining what me and my best friend had. You know that some things in my life don't always end up right. And for you, you're always losing. I guess we kind of sabotaged what we had on purpose, but absentmindedly. You ever thought about that?"

"So, what now? How do we fix this? I'm tired of the back and forth. I'm tired of our mean streaks just to see who can hurt one another the most with what we say or do. Baby, I'm done with this competition of spilling crimson. This the last time we're going to stitch each other up. I promise."

"It was Damon," Cherie said suddenly.

Lazily, Shane lifted his head to look at her. He squinted while studying her face. Was she serious? "The married stripper nigga for a kid?"

Shamefully, Cherie nodded.

"Oh, now she wants her baby to come out and slide from a pole, Jesus!"

"Shane, shut up!" she squealed.

"This baby gon' be throwin' that ass in a circle!"

"Shane!"

"It's gon' come out askin' where the big dollars at!"

Playfully, she smacked his cheek as she giggled. "You can be a real asshole."

"I know." With his hands gripping her waist, he pulled her up so that her face was hovering over his. "You know… when it comes down to it… it's always been about us. Us gettin' it right. Us coming together as one finally. But we shouldn't have any fear in doing it."

"The love's always been there," she mumbled.

"We're tainted as fuck, but it's up to us to clean it up. We've had plenty of casualties in the mix, too."

"We have."

"I'll make you a deal. We both remain on our best behavior with the mindset of being friends, but we still enter a relationship… while not thinking of it being a relationship. It's like trying to be in a relationship kills everything for us. So let's try that? Huh?"

"You know that I love you, right?" Cherie's voice quivered. "I love you so much that it makes me almost resent it because we never last. I love you so much that it hurts me so damn good."

"Stop, Rie. Don't cry."

"You don't understand what you mean to me. When you say hurtful shit, it cuts deeper than anything anybody else can say or do to me. I let you get away with a lot of shit."

"I'm sorry, babe."

"You ain't sorry yet, Shane. We're going to make this work because

I'm tired of the back and forth, too. The next time we end… that's just going to be it."

He kissed her full on the lips. "I don't plan on ending anytime soon."

———————

With Miracle still at Joyce's, Shane rose at seven in the morning accidentally. Since he was already up, he whipped open his bedroom curtains, annoying Cherie on purpose with as long as they stayed up the night prior. She squirmed underneath the thick comforter, dressed in one of Shane's undershirts. He smirked at her as he backed into the master bathroom. As luck would have it, he lined his toothbrush with toothpaste, hearing his phone ring aloud on his nightstand.

Highly irritated, Cherie grabbed his phone when she saw that it was Rich calling. "What?" she asked him with a hiss in his voice. "Do I sound like I'm willing to tell you who the fuck this is? It's a Sunday morning, and you're calling why? Didn't you just get engaged? Like, you're supposed to be asleep from fucking all night, man."

Shane raised a brow at her. She had the audacity to answer his phone when it could've been about work. He made a mental note to let her know not to do that shit again.

Cherie tossed his phone to the foot of the bed, then pulled the covers over her head. "Tell Rich to call you in four hours, after we've gotten enough sleep."

"What's up?" he greeted Rich.

"Yo, I did something bad, fam." Rich was panicking. Shane could tell with how his voice was uneven.

"Slow up. What's up? What happened?"

"Fam… it's bad. Real bad. I don't want to talk about it over the phone. You got to get to my spot. Get here, *now*!"

"I'm on my way. Be cool." Shane hung up and set his phone on top of his chest of drawers.

"You're on your way where?" Cherie grumbled from under the covers.

Shane continued to rummage through his drawers for something to throw on. "I got to get to Rich. He's in a panic."

"Bring me back some coffee, please?"

"Hazelnut brew with extra foam. Got it."

Cherie pulled the covers over her head and sat up in the bed with a contorted face. "Excuse me?" She scowled. "Is that almighty Shane getting something wrong about Cherie, finally?"

"Is that Cherie being bourgeoisie by referring to herself in the third person?" Shane buttoned his designer John Elliott's sweatpants that were knit of black and white with a wool-blend mélange and styled with a slight drop rise.

She scoffed. "I know you're not calling me bourgeoisie when you can't dress down without pulling on a designer, sir."

"Don't mock my sweatpants. Besides, they match my Yeezys."

"Mmhhmm, but I'm the one who's uppity."

Shane went into his closet to grab a white t-shirt with a huge, black Timberland logo on the front, along with his trainers so that he could slide them on.

"By the way," he said over his shoulder, "I know it's Venti Caffe Mocha with extra foam."

"And how would you know that when you've never seen me drink coffee, Shane?" she asked him with squinted eyes.

"Erykah has made me go on plenty runs for her or has had my boys do it. She likes her shit straight black. You're the only other person who works there, so... you know. But you told me to stop knowing you. Getting one wrong for the cause isn't so bad."

She rolled her eyes and laid back down.

"I'm out of here. See you in a little bit." He crawled across the bed and pecked her forehead.

"Babe!" she called when he was close enough to his bedroom door. "You're forgetting something."

"What?"

She lazily pointed to the dresser at his jewelry box. "Black link bracelet would look good with that, and a set of black rosaries."

A smile crept across his face. "Thanks, Rie. I almost forgot."

"And Shane?"

"Yes, babe?"

"Don't get into trouble with Rich. I would hate to have to pull rank after you said to keep in mind that we're friends. I don't feel like being a bitch today."

Without saying another word, he slipped on his jewelry and headed out of the door to see what the issue could've been.

Twelve years ago...

Shane picked his teeth with a toothpick. Since Michelle had gotten her income tax refund late, she thought it would better benefit her son more than her. She had yet to tell him about the possibility of being adopted by the kingpin that was Apollo. Michelle prayed that Apollo would really show up because this was considered the last of their earnings before she would admit herself into a nursing home. Shane was stuffed with hot wings that he had ordered for him and Rich during their lunch period.

Rich, on the other hand, had something that he really needed to tell his buddy. Shane knew so by the way that Rich kept chewing on his bottom lip and on the inside of his jaw.

"What's up?" Shane asked him.

"What... what you mean?" Rich stammered. "Somebody told you that somethin' was up?"

"No, fool." Shane plucked his toothpick across the table at him. "You look nervous as hell. What's on your mind?"

"Dude..." Rich leaned across the table as he looked from side to side to make sure that the cousins— Cherie and Mandy— were nowhere in sight. "I fucked Mandy, bro."

Shane sat back in his seat with a blank expression on his face.

"I'm not playin' with you right now, kid. She came over, I had to give my little brothers five bucks a piece to get them out of the house, and shit—"

"So… why you paranoid?"

"Because!" Rich covered his mouth after his outburst. "I didn't want to be with her, but I don't know if that's how she's feelin'. It was our first time, bruh. How would my mama feel if she knew that I was out here fuckin'? Hmm? She would probably cut my thing off and kick it around on the ground."

"Just chill. Talk to her about it."

"That's easy for you to say because Rie ain't as loud or as crazy as Mandy, man. Besides, y'all niggas probably fuck like rabbits when we ain't around."

"That's what you think?"

"Nigga, it's what I know."

"One, nigga, I'm twelve. I ain't fuckin' nothin' until Rie is ready, which won't be any time soon. Two, you should've waited. Make fun of me all you want, but her body ain't even done developing. Where's the fun in that? You might as well look at yourself like a pedophile because you fucked a kid, with your nasty ass."

"We're the same age!"

"And? That's how I keep myself in check. I ain't a damn pedophile, so I ain't fuckin' no kids."

"You ain't helpin'." Rich waved him off as he leaned back in his seat."

"Yes, I am," Shane chuckled. "You strap up, right? Coach passes out condoms like he expects us to be humpin' in our free time."

"Of course, I strapped. I ain't collected all them condoms since the first day of school for nothin'."

"Then I'm not understandin' why you're panickin'."

"Shane… I don't want to be tied down," he confessed with a serious look on his face. "I been dry-humpin' the shit out of girls, and fingerin' the fuck out of 'em, too. I enjoy gettin' my dick sucked and yanked. I can't do that with a girlfriend. Just one girl? Where's the excitement in that? She's gonna come over here all in love and shit, and I won't be able to shake her."

"Like I said, you should've waited. But I tell you what. How about, if she wants you to be in a relationship, I'll break the news to her with you in the same room? That way, if she wants to fuck you up, I can play referee *and* mediator."

"I knew you were my nigga for a reason." Rich reached over the table to slap five with his homie.

Cherie and Shane might've had one hell of a connection, but Shane and Rich had an unbreakable brotherhood.

CHAPTER SEVEN

What Is Broken

There was no time to waste when Shane hopped out of the Jag and ran up the steps to Rich's front door. He started to knock until he remembered his key. In a hurry, he unlocked the front door and barged in. As soon as he looked to his left inside Rich's living room, he found his old friend on the couch with his palms pressing into his eyes.

"What the hell?" Shane asked with a stressed expression etched onto his face. He looked for blood droplets or a nick, cut, or bruise somewhere on Rich's naked torso as he stood. "What's up? What was the emergency?"

On the hardwood steps, a set of feet came pattering down. Shane turned around just in time to see Mandy lean into the entryway with a smile on her face.

"I'll call you when I make it home, Richard," she said, then scurried to the door. "Bye, Shane!" she called over her shoulder.

Shane turned to Rich with a hard face as the front door opened and closed.

"Bro—"

"You lost your motherfuckin' mind?" Shane bellowed. "You better not tell me that you cheated on my sister, nigga. Your next couple of words to me had better not be that you fucked around and fucked Amanda!"

"We were drunk when we left the spot last night, you know that. Shit, had it not been for Quita and Erykah, we might not have gotten home. We tossed back the same amount of shots—"

"Nah, nigga. The difference between me and you is that I didn't fuckin' propose last night only to end up in bed with somebody that didn't belong to me. You cheated on my sister, folk?"

"I didn't mean to, bro! All I remember is textin' Lyssa to let her know that I was goin' to bed. I woke up next to Mandy and don't remember shit about contactin' her at all last night. You got to help me. Think, Shane! I swear I didn't mean to do this shit! You know I love, Alyssa. If I didn't, I wouldn't have proposed. I don't want her to find out, man. That would crush the fuck out of her, and she would leave me. I love her too much."

"Where the fuck was your love for my sister when you decided to dip into Mandy?"

"I told you, I don't remember shit."

Shane paced as he tapped his thumb against his chin. "You got to tell her."

"You crazy?" Rich shrieked. "Did I forget to mention that she'll kill me *and* Mandy if I told her?"

"Nah, she'll just fuck you up real good, but she won't kill you."

"Shane!"

"I'm dead-ass. You might as well get ready for it because I can't keep this from my sis, bruh. Now you put me in a tight fuckin' position because she's not only my sister, but she's my little sister. My job is to look after her. So you should understand why it is that I can say fuck the 'bro code' right now. She's more important to me than that. If you want, we can take it old school, and I'll be in the same room when you tell her… but don't expect for me to play referee for you. As far as Mandy, I'll have Rie talk to her so she'll keep her mouth closed."

"You think it'll work?"

"Shit, it better. Besides, I know you really love Lyssa. You weren't all bubbly-eyed over Mandy like you are with Lyssa. But let me ask you a question. You cheat on Lyssa before this?"

"Fuck kind of question is that?" Rich yelled. He was highly offended at the question. "This is the first time I've proposed to anybody, and you know that shit! Would I have come to you as a man to ask you to trust me with your sister if I planned on cheatin'? Nigga, I'm your bro! I know you're crazy as fuck, and if dealin' with you is what I had to do in order to fix this situation is what I was going to have to do, then so be it. Shit, I would rather deal with you than to deal with my woman."

Shane shook his head as he pulled out his phone. He didn't know how they would fix this; he only had a hunch. Things were about to get a hell of a lot rockier.

Cherie rolled over at the buzz of her phone on the nightstand next to her. She groaned and prayed that it wasn't Shane telling her that she couldn't get her coffee. Unfortunately, it was her cousin. She didn't want to answer because she needed her sleep, but maybe it was an emergency.

"Yes?" she answered with a huff.

"Cousin! Get up!" Mandy cheered. "I'm on my way to the condo."

"I'm at the house on Clinton Avenue."

"House? The one that Shane made for you?"

"Yes."

"I need the address."

"4212 Clinton Avenue. Zip code 23227."

"Gotcha! Get up, sleepyhead. I have some amazing news!"

Cherie hung up and rolled her eyes. Whatever Mandy was talking about had better been worth her getting out of bed without her coffee.

Shortly after getting herself together, she went down to the living room and waited for her cousin's knock. Her breasts were sore for some reason, so she chose not to wear a bra. She made a mental note to ask Shane for a personal massage. Her lower back and thighs were killing her.

The knock she had been waiting on finally thundered off throughout the house. She made her way to it and pulled the door open. Mandy slammed into her when she hugged her cousin. Cherie had to unlatch her arms from around her cousin. Cherie's abdomen was very tender.

"You okay?" Mandy asked her as she scanned her for a sign of a bruise of some kind.

"I'm just sensitive this morning, that's all," Cherie returned. "Let me go and get a blanket. I'm kind of cold."

Mandy shut the door behind her with her brows furrowed. "Are you about to start your period, Rie? You know some of us are temporarily anemic when we are about to come on."

"Oh, no," Cherie sarcastically sang. "I've only had a period since about fourteen, so, of course, I wouldn't know what my cycle is like."

"You don't have to be an ass about it."

Cherie fetched a blanket out of the hall closet on the second level, wrapped it around her, and showed Mandy to the kitchen where she put the kettle on the stove to brew some herbal tea.

"Mon Cherie Anton," Mandy gushed as she took a seat on the bar stool at the island. "I love your touch on this place. Aunt Davetta said that you were remodeling it before Shane came home. Time really flies, doesn't it?"

"First off, don't be saying my government like we don't have the same last name." Cherie giggled as she took her seat across from her cousin. "Other than that, what's up kid? What's the news?"

"Before I get to that, I want you to know that, when Aunt Davetta is bored, she spills everybody's business. How come you didn't tell me that she ran into Terry a couple months back?"

"Because I didn't find it as anything entertaining. What's she doing tell you that shit for?"

"I don't know? She tells me that he's been missing you. She says he has a house somewhere and has even opened up another company. The legit way this time."

"Oh God." Cherie rolled her eyes. "Why the fuck would he move to Virginia? See, this is the shit that I be talkin' about. Why do people want to act like the man that claims me isn't out of his goddamn marbles? He's calm and content until somebody fucks with him. It's always been that way. Then it's always *'Cherie, come and get Shane because he's swinging from the fucking rafters and slashing throats!'* But fuck that. Don't bother the damn monster if he ain't bothering you. All I'm going to say about that situation is that I hope Terry keeps his distance like he's been doing. Let Shane hear that shit and it's going down. My baby can't stand Terry's ass."

"Girl, who can stand Terry? But it's like I told auntie: Leave that man where he is and stop talkin' to him."

"I told her ass the same shit the day Shane and April were about to get married."

Mandy shook her head and braided the ends of her long ponytail over her shoulder. "My good news though. I fucked Rich last night."

Cherie's face fell flat as her left brow cocked. "Come again?"

"I fucked Rich," Mandy sang happily. "We could be getting back together."

"Two problems with what you just said, Mandy. One… I sat at the family dinner last night to celebrate his engagement to Shane's sister Alyssa."

Mandy's smile was completely wiped off. The news had hit her so hard that she immediately stopped braiding her hair.

"Two... you know I love you... but Rich already ditched you. It took you a year to get over that. You don't want to step back into something so poisonous."

"Poisonous?" she breathlessly asked. "Like you and Shane?"

"Come on now, don't do that. Every situation is different. We know what we have, and we know that we've done some pretty fucked up shit to one another, so don't compare you and Rich to us."

"No, let it be said, Rie. If it's not about you and Shane then it's just not right."

"I never said that, and I think you need to calm down. If you want to go over there and get burned by the man who's engaged to my sister-in-law then, by all means, carry yourself over there."

"I'm so disappointed in you right now."

"Me?"

"You've been avoiding Shane and then sulk over him when he moves on, but I was still there for you."

"Actually, you weren't. Need I remind you that you went out on a double-date with Jessica?"

"That has nothing to do with it."

"You know what's funny? Shane called me self-righteous and spoiled last night. That's you. You think that just because you stay tight-lipped about shit that it's really not happening. Mandy, I'm not going to kiss your ass because you've heard the truth. I would've been a fucked-up person if I kept Rich's engagement from you. But let's take it back to when I first got to fucking Virginia. You have been in constant contact with me and Shane, and not once have you opened your mouth to either one of us about what was going on. You knew I was engaged and didn't tell him, even though you knew he loved me. You knew that he was with my own sister before I got back, but you never told me."

"It wasn't my business or my place to, Cherie!"

"Oh, it wasn't?"

"No!"

"Then what a fucked-up person you really are. And then you sit here like it's okay for me to keep shit from you that I know about."

"It was probably an elaborate rouse to—"

"Ouch!" Cherie doubled over the island with her forearm pressed inside her abdomen.

Mandy jumped back. "Rie, are you okay?"

"Yea," she said lowly. "Probably just a menstrual cramp or something."

As soon as Mandy tilted her head to say something else, Cherie took in a sharp breath.

"Okay, I don't think you're okay, Rie."

"I just need some Tylenol…" Cherie sat frozen on the stool when feeling a little flutter at the bottom of her stomach.

"Rie?" Fear flooded Amanda as she cautiously rounded the island.

If her pain wasn't enough, Cherie felt something warm trickle down her leg. "Call Shane," she told her cousin with a low and shaky voice.

"Rie?"

A lone and frightful tear trickled down the side of her face as the realization hit her of the inevitable. "Mandy... call Shane."

CHAPTER EIGHT

Asking And Receiving

When Mandy called Davetta, she took an Uber to the hospital to find her daughter. Her heart was broken into pieces when hearing that something had happened to her child. Out of all the things that had happened between them, she was a changed person. She was devoted to trying her best to repair the things that were broken between her and Cherie. Because Mandy gave no details, Davetta was in a complete panic.

She stopped in her tracks when she was face to face with the image of another woman sitting on the side of her daughter's bed, holding her hand and stroking her cheek. She wondered who the woman was when she ended the prayer and tried to get up, but Cherie wouldn't let her go.

"Mama, please?" Cherie begged. It was a stab at Davetta. Hearing Cherie call someone else "mama" hurt her to her core. "I'm scared," Cherie continued. "I don't know what they're going to do to me."

"Your man is right here, baby," Joyce told her lovingly. "He's going to be with you through it all. You know I have to go to be with the little ones out in the waiting room."

"What?"

"I hope that you didn't think that your family wasn't going to come and see about you."

"Speaking of family," Davetta spoke up. She ventured over to the bed and purposely grabbed Cherie's hand out of Joyce's, then looked Joyce square in the eyes. "Who are you?"

Joyce raised a brow at Davetta's disrespect. "I'm Joyce," she told her as she folded her arms. "You must be Cherie's biological womb donor."

"I am, and you ain't got no business lettin' her call you my name."

Cherie snatched her hand out of her mother's. "Don't come in here—"

"Davetta, you're going to have to wait in the waiting room," Shane said from behind her. "They're only letting one person in here at a time. Cherie doesn't need to be stressed. You got a problem with my mama, then you need to tell me."

"Boy, your mama's name is Michelle," Davetta angrily spewed. "I don't know who this woman is, but she damn sure ain't Chelle."

"You would know what happened if you were around instead of treating Cherie like your meal ticket. Now, please... take your seat in the waiting room."

Davetta rolled her eyes and snarled at Joyce before taking her leave. The woman had a lot of nerve to try and come in and take her place. She damn near bumped into Josiah on her way out. Even he received the evil eye.

"Baby girl, are you alright?" he asked, paying Davetta no attention.

Shane stopped him before he could get to the bed. Joyce patted his shoulder as she took her leave for sympathy.

"Josiah, when I promised to take care of your daughter, I should've asked which one, huh?"

Though the joke was inappropriate, Josiah lightly chuckled anyhow.

"Listen, Cherie's had a serious miscarriage, and she won't let the doctors or nurses touch her. Please do what you do as a father to get her to kind of calm down a little bit. They're going to have to put something in her IV pretty soon. I mean, if this was Miracle and I was standing in your place, I would be shaking in my boots."

Josiah nodded accordingly, then moved past Shane to give his daughter some comforting words. A nurse appeared in the doorway and fingered for Shane to come to her in the hall. He obliged, hoping for some kind of good news.

"Mr. Hartford, I've looked around for what you asked for," she informed him. "It appears that we do have pamphlets that explain the procedure and why it's so important for her to have it."

"Yea, but I don't think that'll work," he replied. "Maybe if y'all can explain it to her very gently, then she would let you do what you need to do, as opposed to y'all having to ambush her to knock her out."

"Yes, sir. The doctor is on his way back now, and we'll do what we can to distract her to give her a sedative in her IV."

"I like how you think, Nurse," he chuckled. "I'll go in here and talk her down a little."

"Thank you for your cooperation, Mr. Hartford."

"No problem, Miss."

Shane went back into the room, just as Josiah was coming out.

"Baby, they're going to take the baby," Cherie cried.

"No, no, babe," he told her sympathetically. He reached her and kneeled beside the bed to stroke her short locks. "Your body couldn't handle it, baby, so it didn't survive. That's all. It's no need to be ashamed of it."

"But, my baby…"

"It's okay, Rie. We'll have another, okay, baby?"

"It's already here, Shane," she whined.

"It's not, baby," he said softly. "It went back to God. He wanted his sweet angel back."

"He knew that I wanted it."

"I know. Some things just aren't meant to be. But I promise you that after this, we'll try as hard as we need to just to get another one, okay?"

"I want my baby back!"

Shane curled his arms around her shaking shoulders to hold her. He knew that it hurt her more than anything to first be oblivious to the fact that she had even conceived, and secondly, it hurt not to have what she had always wanted.

"The nurse said that I was eight weeks," she sniffled. "It was your baby, Shane."

He slowly and gently wiped away the gloss from her cheeks. "I knew that your little sneaky self didn't want to stop riding me the day you were wearing that jersey in my bed. I just didn't say anything because you didn't. Other than that, I assumed that you were on birth control. That was another reason I was shocked when you told me that you were on fertility drugs."

"I didn't have sex with Damon after you if that's what you're wondering."

"Of course, I wouldn't have thought that."

"Good evening, Ms. Anton!" a strong voice called from the doorway.

Shane moved over to the other side of the bed out of courtesy.

The tall, brown skinned man closed Cherie's chart within his massive hands and took her hand into his own. "I heard that you were afraid of the procedure," he said soothingly. "Is that why you're kicking up a fuss down here? Is that why I was called in?"

"I was trying so hard," Cherie informed him with a shaky voice.

"Is it okay if I give you a few facts that I've picked up along the way?"

Slowly, she nodded.

"Unfortunately, miscarriage is the most common type of natural pregnancy loss. Anywhere from ten to twenty-five percent of clinically recognized pregnancies will end in miscarriage, and most miscarriages occur during the first thirteen weeks of pregnancy. I know that it can be such an exciting time when pregnant, but with the number of miscarriages that occur, it is beneficial to be informed in the unfortunate event that you face one. Now, the reason that people are telling you all of this mumbo jumbo is because the main goal of treatment during or after a miscarriage is to prevent hemorrhaging and/or infection. The earlier you are in your pregnancy, the more likely your body will expel all the fetal tissue by itself and will not require further medical procedures. If the body does not expel all the tissue, the most common procedure performed to stop bleeding and prevent infection is a D and C. I know that you were trying your best to conceive, Mon Cherie, but this is what we're facing. Let's just say that your body didn't want to let the baby go either. So now we have to go in and get it before any more damage can be done to you that may prevent another pregnancy."

"What... what is this D and C?"

"A D and C is actually the abbreviation of dilation and curettage. It's a surgical procedure often performed after a first-trimester miscarriage. In a D and C, dilation refers to opening the cervix; curettage refers to removing the contents of the uterus. Curettage may be performed by scraping the uterine wall with a curette instrument or by a suction curettage." He then leaned down to her ear and whispered, "Let's just say it's a vacuum." He then winked at her with a polite smile dressing his face.

"Do I have to do this? It sounds like I'm getting an abortion."

"Oh, no. Abortions are different. We're not taking a life. We're basically cleaning out your uterus. Some women can easily miscarry with no issue, but as I've said, there are still tissues that need to be removed. We have anesthesia and antibiotics for you. It won't be a bother. This is what I call the easy part, Ms. Anton. You see, my wife has had four miscarriages before we finally got the chance to say hello to our first little bundle of joy. Then, of course, after the first came four more. Now the first three are in college, and we still have two more at home."

"It sounds easy for you."

"It wasn't. The procedure itself is easy, but my wife fell into a very deep depression, she questioned God, we had to see a doctor about fertility to put her mind at ease, and we almost divorced. My best advice would be to seek professional counseling or therapy afterward. The body can heal on its own, sometimes needing a little help. The heart and mind, however, need a little more help than the body. So, my question to you is, are you ready? Are you ready to walk through the storm and prepare for your next blessing?"

Cherie looked over at Shane, and the tears erupted on their own.

He leaned over and hugged her as tightly as he could. He turned his head toward the doctor and nodded so that the nurse could come in and give Cherie her anesthesia.

———

Joyce adjusted the covers up to Cherie's chest as she lay on the canopy bed. Josiah stood in the doorway, while Erykah and Ashington sat on the other side of the bed.

"Is that good enough for you, baby?" Joyce asked sweetly.

"Yes," she answered with a raspy voice. "Can I get some water?"

"I'll get it!" Ashington volunteered.

Joyce leaned down and pecked Cherie's forehead while Davetta stood in the corner of the master bedroom. "Quita wants you to know that she's sorry she couldn't be here. She had a wedding party to get ready for tomorrow. She says she doesn't know who the hell would want their wedding on a Monday, but she really is sorry."

"It's alright." Cherie forced a small smile. With the pain meds in her system, it was a miracle that she was even speaking. "Where are the kids?"

"King is down for a nap," Erykah told her.

"And Miracle?"

Shane stepped forward with his daughter on his arm. She had already fallen asleep at nine o'clock at night. Gently, Shane laid her next to Cherie on his pillow and watched as Cherie cuddled up next to his toddler, shut her eyes, and finally drifted off to sleep.

Afterward, everyone exited the room, including Davetta. She stopped Shane at the bottom of the steps with a more than serious look on her face. "Don't you ever have my baby callin' another woman 'mama', do you understand me? It's alright for you because you ain't my son, so I can't tell you what to do. But Mon Cherie is my child."

Shane removed her hand from his Timberland shirt, taking a step away from the agile woman. "I'll have you know that my mama has been more of a mama to Cherie than you have in all twenty-five years of her life. Also, don't ever touch me, Davetta. I don't like to be touched."

"Oh, you hear this, *Joyce*?" Davetta whirled around to the woman, who was standing near the door with her own daughter and grandson. "You hear the way your son is speaking to me?"

Joyce folded her arms as she gulped. Davetta was a few years late to the party to think that she hadn't dealt with Davetta's kind before. "Davetta, is it? Please don't try and turn things around on my son. You hear me? Yes, he's my son because I raised him after Michelle did a wonderful job with him. Thanks to her, may she rest in peace, it wasn't a difficult job to accomplish. Yes, my stepchildren and honorary children have the privilege of calling me their mother, because that's who I am. They cry to me, I uplift them, they confide in me, and mostly, I've kept them away from their father's wrath when I could. Pardon me because I just so happen to be better at it than you. Now stop all of this showboating for attention before I have to put somethin' hot on your ass."

"Somethin' hot, huh? Like what, lil' Joyce?"

"Davetta, you need to calm down and get out of my house," Shane warned her. "All of this foolishness is unnecessary."

"Well don't have my kid callin' this bitch her mama!"

"And this..." Joyce calmly stated with a smile. "This is exactly why they get to call me their mom and not you. You don't know how to act in damn public. Remove yourself from my son's home."

"I hope your son is prepared for my daughter to go back home to her husband. Because after all of this bullshit? That's exactly where she's headed."

"Mama, hold King," Erykah said as tried to pry her young one off her shoulder.

"No, no," Joyce stopped her. "It won't be anyone fighting in my son's home. Not today there won't. Unlike her, we know where Cherie belongs. And for her to even say something like that, it proves how much she's not even close to being in the know. Davetta, your daughter just lost my son's baby. If she was going back to little old Terry, she would've done that damn near two years ago. Let me say this one more time before I have to reach into my nice Gucci handbag for something that'll make you dance… and I'm not speaking of cash, my dear. Leave. My. Son's. *Home.*"

Davetta rolled her eyes and squeezed past Joyce and Erykah in front of the door. Before she left, she just had to get the last word in. "You know, Shane," she began, with narrowed lids that barely hid her icy eyes. "You've always been a heathen. A low-life, slum crawling heathen. You don't stand a damn chance against a man… a *real* man… like Terry."

Shane watched her as she walked out of the front door and slammed it behind her. He didn't take her words to heart. Instead, he sent his family away and did his duties as an unofficial husband. He prepared chicken noodle soup from scratch, then made Cherie a jug of lemonade for whenever her pain medication wore off and she would have a hankering for something. Afterward, he went back up to his suite, showered, and crawled into bed with both his heartbeats. His woman and his daughter.

Cherie stirred a little, then finally reached her right hand behind her to feel that Shane was near. "What time is it?" she grumbled.

"It's ten o'clock, babe," he lowly returned.

"You're in bed this early? Don't you have something to do?"

"Yea. I have to be right here with you." Gently, he curved his arm over her waist and squeezed her stomach a little. Hearing her only shudder, he kissed her shoulder. "We'll get it right one day, Rie," he quietly promised. "You have the house, the car, the man… you're just missing the resort and spa, and of course, the baby. We never got around to talking about that, you know."

"What do you mean?" Cherie squeezed her brows together.

"Seventh grade… Home Ec… the project we did together. You had your whole life planned out in that binder of yours and on that poster board. I had promised to give you everything you wanted… but we never got around to the kids part."

Cherie lowly giggled when thinking of it, even though it hurt her stomach to do so. "I remember that day. Mandy was giving Rich the blues because they had triplets and he stuck her in a, umm…"

"Buick."

"Right. And you offered to give them money."

"Yup. And we never got around to discussing the kids. You wanted twins."

"With different color eyes."

"And you wanted all their names to sound the same."

"Yea. You got mad at me because we were five years into our marriage and I had yet to put kids in our project."

"So, what do you want? Do you want to get married and wait five years? Or do you want to start six weeks from now? It's up to you."

"Right now... I want to go back to sleep."

"Fine." Shane pecked her shoulder before sliding out of bed. He retrieved Miracle so that he could take her into her own room, undress her, and made sure that she didn't need to be changed again. She would be starting to potty train soon, so he had to keep tabs on things like that. Shane knew that having Miracle changed him, so he really had to ask himself if he were ready for more children.

CHAPTER NINE

Standing Up and Falling Down

When Shane finally let Cherie out of the house, the first thing she did was go to her condo with Mandy in tow. She hadn't forgotten about how rude Mandy was when hearing the truth about Rich and his engagement, yet she let it slide due to the fact that her cousin jumped into action when something was wrong. To make it all one trip, she called Quita and had her to come along since she took a day off from the shop.

As soon as they stepped into the condo, Cherie could've passed out at the man she saw on the couch. Sitting with his legs crossed in a pair of jeans and a V-neck t-shirt was Terry. He looked to be comfortable there. A little too comfortable. She squinted at him and placed her hand on her hip. Quita stumbled over the threshold, almost bumping into her sister-in-law. She had to follow the little woman's line of sight to see what could've made her stop in her tracks.

"Oh, hell no!" Mandy exclaimed. She moved Cherie aside and took off her trucker cap that she only wore to hide her unattended roots. "Why the fuck are you in my cousin's house, my dude?" Mandy clapped along with her sentence, then threw her purse to the hardwood floor. "Where the fuck is Aunt Davetta?"

"Umm... Rie?" Quita leaned over to Cherie as her eyes darted from Cherie to Terry. "Who is this man in your house, and why does he look like he belongs here? Do I need to call my brother or take off my earrings? I'm with you, bitch. *All* the way."

"You're not going to say hello to your fiancé?" Terry rubbed his hands together, wearing a sly smile on his chocolate-colored face. "You haven't seen me—"

"Since you were with *your* fiancée at my jewelry show in California," Cherie interrupted him.

"And you been juicin' my auntie for info?" Mandy asked. There was a squeal at the tail-end of her sentence as she squatted to meet Terry at eye level from across the room. "I knew you were a sneaky nigga but comin' off up in my cousin's spot, though?"

"I'm trippin' because he called himself your fiancé," Quita remarked. "Does he not know who my brother is?"

Terry slowly stood and casually slid his hands into his pockets. He wasn't threatened by Mandy being ready to pounce on him, or Quita waiting for Cherie's words to dial Shane. He wasn't close to being bothered by the scowl on Cherie's face. "Your brother?" he questioned. "You mean, the dude who has nothing better to do than to steal other men's women? The dude who peddles drugs to Virginians? He's nothing compared to me, baby."

Quita stepped forward, but Cherie stretched her arm out in front of her. "Don't even," she said. "He's nothing but my mama's gossip partner. He's a bitch in a man's skin. He's nothing to worry about."

"That's how you feel, Cherie?"

"Yea. Exactly how I feel. For the record, you bring Shane into anything else, and it's gonna be me and you… *Terrance.*"

"Cherie?"

All heads turned to Davetta as she strolled into the condo with a few grocery bags in her hands. She was dressed comfortably in a pair of black leggings with a matching tank top. Davetta made Cherie want to gag at her attire. Davetta must've wanted to woo Terry with her form-fitting attire because she had never worn anything of the sort before.

"Why the hell are you threatening Terry?" she asked as she closed the door behind her. "He came here as my guest."

"Didn't I tell you to stop talking to him?" Cherie worked her neck.

"He came by because he had some important news for me about an investment. After all, you've shot him down and changed your number."

"That's because he got me into some serious trouble with the government and the fucking Chinese mafia!"

"He's seen the error of his ways, Mon Cherie."

"You keep believing that. And since the both of you are so fucking comfy-cozy, you keep me out of all of your shit. That's your new homie…" Cherie stopped in the middle of her sentence, just to closely eye her mother. "And I'm guessing that he's your soon to be man… so keep y'all shit where y'all sleep."

"Cherie!"

She fanned them off and took her leave to her room so that she and her girls could pack what they could in a short amount of time.

"You got fuckin' lucky," Mandy said. She made a handgun gesture at him as she passed to let him know that his time was coming soon.

After a while of tossing articles of clothing inside of luggage and boxes, Terry gently knocked on the pane of her bedroom door. All the women snarled at him when they noticed him standing in the doorway.

"Fuck you want?" Mandy harshly asked him. She was sitting on the floor in front of her cousin's dresser while emptying it out.

"I need to speak to Mon Cherie alone, please," he politely told them all.

"Fuck that! My cousin doesn't want to speak to you—"

"Was I asking your ratchet ass for permission?"

"Nigga, you have a serious problem with hearing," Quita spat from in front of the massive walk-in closet. "I'm glad that I keep insurance for niggas like you."

"Insurance, huh? Well, I'm glad that I keep something to put in the mouths of bitches like you."

"And what you gon' be puttin' in my sister's mouth?"

Cherie's heart dropped. Quita smirked as she folded her arms. Mandy slowly stood and backed into the wall near the bed. Terry himself had to stand frozen in place because of the breath at the back of his neck. Quita had sent a 9-1-1 text to Shane to tell him to get to Cherie's condo because they felt unsafe without another man near. It was all hockey, but she did the right thing. Had Shane known that something had gone down without any one of them letting him know, they would've been in some serious trouble with him and his temper.

Slowly, Terry turned his head to the side.

"I asked you a question," Shane said through closed teeth. "What the fuck you say to my sister?"

"Listen, Shane." Terry pulled a smile onto his face as if not to be bothered. "All I'm saying is, your sister has a very loose mouth. It's not lady-like to speak some of the things that she has spoken to me."

Shane took two steps back, but that didn't mean that he was letting Terry off the hook. If anybody knew him like they were supposed to, then they would've known that it would only take him a millisecond to draw back two years ago and slam his fist into the back of Terry's head. The force sent him stumbling over the threshold of Cherie's room. Mandy was only lucky enough to hop up onto Cherie's bed before joining Quita and her cousin in front of the closet.

The girls were hushed. They knew what it was like when Shane was upset. No one dared to intervene. Even Davetta shuffled to the doorway to see what was happening, but she remained quiet and in shock.

Terry turned around to try and defend himself, yet he didn't count on being grabbed by the throat, lifted into the air, or being slammed onto his back on the floor. Shane wasn't done by a long shot. With his temper at an all-time high, he took his size fourteen sneakers to Terry's ribs and arms. He had had enough of Terry. If he had it his way, he would've disfigured the man's face with his feet. Terry, however, could've sworn that there were more people in the room stomping the life out of him because Shane's feet were coming down and cracking bones so quickly.

Cherie stood idly by with her heart racing as the thumps, grunts, and inaudible words filled the room. She knew that Shane was a maniac, but she was starting to question if she should've stopped what was happening.

When thinking of all the acidic words Terry spat over the last two years, all the things he had done and all the trouble he caused, Shane pulled his nine millimeter from underneath his shirt, behind his back. Quickly, he snapped the top of it to load his bullets into the chamber and pointed it directly at Terry.

"Babe!" Cherie blurted. "Baby, don't. Just… that's enough. Let someone find him in the hospital parking lot or something."

With a steady arm and his pistol still aimed at Terry, Shane's disheveled face softened when hearing Cherie's voice. "That's the last time she's saving your bitch ass." He then turned around to find Davetta standing there in the doorway. The corner of his top lip rose as he eyed her in disgust. "And this is the bitch nigga that you wanted to marry your daughter?"

"You just proved how much of an animal you are," Davetta returned through closed teeth. "He has more class than you."

"That'd be true, but I would never put my hands on your daughter, make her my fall-dummy, or fuck her best friend and then marry the bitch."

"You fucked her sister, had a baby with her, and almost married another hoe."

"That's also true, but that bloody and unrecognizable motherfucker on the floor behind me will never be *me*."

Silence fell over the room once more. The women standing at the face of the closet stood in fear. They could feel the tension. It was almost as if Shane was going to slap the shit out of Davetta next.

"Rie," he strongly called her with his eyes still on Davetta. "Fuck all this shit. Leave it right where it is. Only take your documents. I'll get you all new shit. We don't need this negative energy in our home. We're going to leave low life bitches where they stand, which is on a path to live up to their own daughter. Oh, and Davetta. You call me another motherfuckin' low life, animal, or anything that's not my name… and I'm sendin' my *mama* after you, bitch." Shane aggressively bumped into Davetta as he passed on his way to the front door.

Cherie looked at both Quita and Mandy, trying to figure out if it was safe to move just yet.

"Rie!" he bellowed. It made them all flinch. "Have somebody call an ambulance for that pussy ass nigga! Bring y'all ass on before you send me to prison!"

Cherie rolled her eyes. "He always got to be so damn demanding."

"What?"

"Nothing, baby!"

"Then let's go!"

Cherie huffed and tilted her head at Mandy. "Cousin, look in the closet, on the top right shelf. It's an envelope up there somewhere with most of my info in it. And, Quita, grab the luggage that you already packed for me. Davetta, call the ambulance for your bitch. Lastly, you can have this fuckin' condo. It's going to be in your name come Monday morning."

————————

Alas, Shane and Cherie were on a better road. She maintained her ability to keep him calm when needed, and in turn, he escorted her to counseling sessions. The pair had much to do rather than to keep the thought of Terry roaming around Virginia anywhere close to the brain. It had been two weeks since Cherie decided that it was time for her to get back into the saddle to try and make another baby. She ignored Shane's constant complaints of how he wanted to do everything the right way. Whatever that meant.

On her birthday, Cherie woke up alone. She stared at the pillow in front of her and scowled. How or why would Shane leave her lonely on her most cherished day? Her birthday had already started off wrong after all of the planning that had gone into it.

The phone behind her on the nightstand blared Mary J. Blige's song "Stronger". It was Shane calling. He had better have a decent excuse as to why he couldn't be there when she opened her eyes. She rolled over as she brushed her flying bang out of her face so that she could answer for her love.

When she didn't say anything, Shane chuckled. "Don't be so mad. Stop making that face, Rie."

"Why the fuck are you not here? What's so funny?"

"Hey, don't worry about all of that. Get ready to open the door. It's about to be one of the best days of your life."

Cherie stared at her phone when he hung up with her brows squeezing together. Was he serious?

On cue, the doorbell rang. She dragged herself out of bed and galloped down the steps to answer.

Erykah leaned over the threshold with a smile on her face and a cup holder with four cups of coffee in it. "Happy birthday!" she cheered. "Drink this down, and then get all dolled up. Your fun begins *now!*"

Cherie rolled her eyes. "Did your brother put you up to this?"

"You know it. Now come on. We have times to meet and destinations to get to."

"Fine." She closed the door, then took the cup out of the holder that had her name on it with drawn on stars around it.

Cherie took her coffee upstairs with her as she groomed and dressed for the day. Even though the gesture of taking her away for the day was appreciated, she still couldn't believe that Shane had somehow chosen work over her.

Descending the stairs in a pair of navy-blue suede pumps with a steel heel on them, a clinging white tank top, and her large silver mirror tinted shades donning her face, Cherie didn't look like she was happy to be going anywhere.

"Oh, come on, Rie," Erykah sympathetically sang when seeing the straight line that Cherie's lips made. "Don't look so upset. Shane's coming."

"Erykah... he chose to work on *my* day."

"You know he has something in store for later. Just trust me. Fuck him. Trust *me*."

"What does he have up his sleeve, Erykah?"

"You know I can't tell you that. I would love to, but I can't."

Cherie folded her arms. "Tell me or else I'm not leaving."

"Fine. I'll give you a hint. *Eternity*."

"That's all you got for me?"

"That's all I can give you, babes? Now come on. Quita's waiting for us at the salon."

Finally, Cherie surrendered. Getting her hair done wouldn't be something to be mad about.

"You know this is going to get me killed and get you fucked up, right?" Shane asked Rich. "It's Rie's birthday. I'm supposed to be with her, not here."

Rich stood from his couch and paced again. His thoughts were all over the place. He was going to have to come out and tell Alyssa what he did one day. Today would be better than any. He knew that she was supposed to be going out with the girls, compliments of his homie, so he thought that Alyssa would want to get in and out and wouldn't have wanted to mess up her attire or her nails.

Shane sat with his ankle relaxing against the opposite knee. Other than being there for his friend, he really did have to work. Rich's confession came at a bad time for everybody.

When the door came open, with the alarm alerting them that it had opened, Rich stopped pacing. Shane could've sworn that he saw

Rich shaking in place.

Alyssa, looking as well as ever, approached her man and wrapped her arms around his neck. She stepped back as she flipped her long and wavy tresses. Alyssa could feel that something was wrong, yet she hoped that whatever the matter could've been would be solved within the next five minutes. She was due for her hair appointment with the girls, then they were off to brunch. She looked over at her brother on the loveseat, knowing for a fact that he had invested too much thought, consideration, and funds into Cherie's special day for her to miss even one event out of the criteria for the day.

"What's going on?" she asked Rich.

Rich, being a coward in the moment, stared at Shane with hope in his eyes.

Shane dropped his phone inside the gap of his legs and cleared his throat. "Lyssa, your boy got drunk a couple of nights ago and did some shit that he really wishes that he could take back. If you ask me, I believe him. You of all people know that I ain't lenient when it comes to anything, and I know when people are telling the truth. He was honest when he basically cried about wishing that he could take it back and how he wasn't present when—"

"Baby, I fucked Mandy," Rich finished. He was looking his woman in the eyes, and he was more than ready to accept his punishment.

Alyssa stepped back as her chest caved.

"Baby—"

"You called me over here when you knew that I had to be there for Rie?" she asked him with disgust in her voice. "You know damn well that we're on a schedule, but you chose today of all days to do this?"

"Lyssa, I'm so sorry," he pleaded. "I didn't mean that shit—"

"Richard, you could've called me or sent that shit to me in a text. Hell, when we were working *yesterday* you could've told me."

"I know, but—"

"Lastly, you're shivering like loose booty meat. Tighten that shit up. I'm not worried about no damn Mandy."

"You're not?" he questioned confusingly.

"No. And, also…" Out of the blue, Alyssa punched Rich so hard and so quick that it took him a minute to feel the impact and realize that he had hit the ground on his side and had frozen in place. Alyssa stood over him and proclaimed, "When this bitch comes to Cherie's party, you'll act like nothing ever happened, you hear me? We're engaged, so you better pretend that you remember that shit. She had better be the only bitch you fucked while you were with me because, if not, I'm fuckin' the both of you up. I know for a fact that she will be the last because I will take your goddamn life if you ever step out on me again."

"Yes, baby," Rich agreed as he frantically nodded. "She was the only one, and it will never happen again."

"I know it better not. You got a grown ass woman who doesn't need fuckin' handouts. Nigga, I clawed my way out of a bad ass life to stand on my own two feet. Oh, but you cheat on me with a hoe who shops at Rainbow and DD's Discount? You cheated on me with a bitch who has to ride her cousin's coattail just to live? Don't you ever downgrade on me again or else I swear I will take your life."

"No, baby, it won't ever happen again. I swear."

With nothing more to say, she left the house, mumbling to herself. "Lost his motherfuckin' mind. Downgrading and shit. Dumb ass nigga."

"Get up," Shane told him as he stood. "You gon' have to wash your face after that shit because you're leakin'. You better be lucky that's all you got because Lyssa ain't got it all."

"None of the Cruzs are sane," Rich commented.

"Stop complainin'. We got to get to the money, and I got to talk to the plugs to make sure they got their eyes on that Terry nigga."

Rich stumbled to his feet with his face contorted. "You still on that shit?"

"*No* nigga comes into my state and makes threats, *period*. I'm done with his ass. Since Cherie doesn't want me to kill his ass, I'm gonna hit him financially. You remember when he threatened my daddy's business, fam. For that... I'm gonna drain his ass. Fuck him."

"Speaking of finances, you need to talk to Bo. He's—"

"Thanks to this memory loss bullshit, I was meaning to talk to you about him. Why the fuck do you have him reportin' to you?"

"Because the books ain't right, bruh. Every time he goes out of town, he's spending company money on booze and bitches. Don't get me wrong, everybody deserves a little wind-down every now and again... but something's wrong with him. I asked him if everything was okay, and he brushed me off. Even worse, I've been having to replace some of your supply. I think he may be using. That's exactly why I have him reporting. I need to know what the hell is going on."

Shane squinted as he listened. Then, he made a note on his phone to go over product a few days from then before Rich could get to it, just to see how much money was being spent and how much product was being used. Something was foul. Bo was like Shane's second father. He should've seen some type of sign that something was going on with him.

CHAPTER TEN

Stuck On You

After a full day of beauty, rejuvenation, and lounging with the girls, Cherie sat with a pout on while everyone at her long table talked among themselves. Occasionally, she would look down at the other end of the table that seated thirty-two people with fifteen on each side, leaving her and Shane at either end. But he wasn't there. He had yet to return her texts or her voicemails. She was beyond steamed. Cherie was mere seconds away from breaking down in tears. It wasn't like him to ignore her for the majority of the day. The last text he sent to her when they had arrived at the Infusion— a nightclub that catered to special events— said that he was still working and had gotten caught up. Even Rich was absent.

However, she did notice the icy stares that Mandy and Alyssa were sharing. She wondered if they knew about one another. Either way, the clients that Cherie earned attended her party, and thank God they knew how to have a good time or else she would've been deeper inside her feelings more than what she was already.

"Presents!" Ashington screamed as she stood. It was apparent that she was a bit tipsy, yet no one said anything. After having to buckle down in her third year of college and staying on the straight and narrow, she deserved to hang loose for a minute. "Come on, y'all! My sister-in-law needs her presents over here!"

Quita stood in her pumps and head gestured for Erykah to follow her so that she could help bring the presents over to the table.

Cherie did what she always did and slapped a smile on while harboring all kinds of feelings that she didn't want anyone to know of.

Mandy took a sip from her champagne glass and said to her cousin, "Shane would've been here if he didn't have to work, Rie. You know that. At least he put you together a pretty good gathering, and we've had fun all day."

"Sister-in-law, my brother will be here. Don't worry about a thing," Alyssa intervened.

"I believe that I was speaking to my cousin."

"You could've been, but then I started talking to her. What's your point?"

"Gifts!" Erykah happily sang to make the other two stop arguing. By no means did she want a gathering of well-dressed people in white end up with blood and weave glue on their attire if Alyssa and Mandy threw physical blows at one another. She placed the first large box on the table in front of Cherie and stepped back.

Happily, Cherie opened the box and gushed at the handcrafted tiara that was especially fit for her.

"You're such a drama queen that I had to make you one," Erykah joked.

"Well, you know me," Cherie giggled.

Erykah fit the tiara on her head while Quita loaded the table with more of Cherie's boxes. With joy, she opened them all and thanked the individuals who had given them to her. By the last box, the feeling of hurt hit her once more. She found herself standing in her black see-through chiffon dress that stopped three inches above her knees and flared in the back. Thankfully, she was wearing a pair of high-waist short shorts or else she really would've had a problem if Shane was there and saw what she had on. She was just about to thank everyone collectively for thinking of her when shopping for gifts when Quita stopped her.

"You have one more gift though, Rie."

"I do?" she quizzed with her head tilted to the side. Her feathery bang fell into her face, yet Cherie hadn't swiped it away.

"Yup, and it's *huge*."

"Y'all got me something big?"

"Well… not necessarily us. You know my brother has to be a showoff."

Cherie rolled her eyes. His name, at this point, made her want to break something.

"You don't want your gift?" a familiar voice ushered the question inside her ear with more baritone that should've been allowed.

Her body lightly shivered as a hand snaked around her waist and landed onto her small pudge.

The guests erupted into their gushes and cheers at the man of the hour who was so close to being murdered that it wasn't even funny.

He turned her around as she tried her best to hide her blush. "Tell me, Rie. You don't want your gift?"

She bit down on her bottom lip, narrowing her eyes at him. He smelled divine, his edge-up was on point, and his attire had him three seconds away from being raped on the party table. Cherie didn't want to compliment Shane in his pressed white slacks, open white dress shirt that revealed his tattoos along his collarbone, or the fact that the shirt had black trims just to try and match her. Even his accessories were silver, just like hers. He wore his dreads in two ponytails over his shoulders that she wanted to pull, but she couldn't because that would lead to other things.

"Where's my gift?" she finally asked as she worked her neck.

"You want it?"

"I mean, you avoided me all day, walk off in here lookin' like you just stepped out of a boutique, but you don't have my gift? Like, what the fu—"

Before Cherie could finish her rant, Shane dropped to one knee.

All the wind had been knocked out of Cherie. She was forced to take a sloppy step backward in her peep-toe, black leather heels. With her bottom lip still caged between her teeth, she covered her mouth with her free hand; the other being held captive; engulfed within Shane's massive palm. This day was really happening. She fantasized about it but never thought that it would've happened. Twice she thought that all hope was lost for them, yet looking down into the gorgeous and pure brown orbs of his, she knew that it was true. Their future was surely bright.

"You know you've been my best friend for a decade and a half, right?" he questioned to begin his speech. "Cherie, all that I am, all of me... De'Shane Hartford... is all of you. You, along with everyone else in this room, are well-aware of the fact. You were once the girl that I had to shelter and protect from almost everything. You grew up to be a self-sufficient woman who rarely ever reaches out to me for a damn thing. You might be hard headed as fuck, but I still love you."

Though tears streamed down her cheeks, she managed to roll her eyes in dismay at his statement. She would've had a comeback for him if her words weren't stuck in her throat.

"You gave me so many happy memories that I could only hope and pray that your answer to my next question is yes," Shane continued. "Will you allow me to live those memories for the rest of my life, and will you be kind enough to let me have my best friend until my last breath? I wish I could pay you back for all the happiness that you've given me, but this will just have to do. So... will you marry me and let me give back what you gave?"

The family and friends were urging Cherie to say yes, but her answer was lodged between the walls of her lungs. When she took in a breath, she had to look over at the table and ask the spectators, "Is he for real? Like, is this really happening?"

"Yes!" Quita cheered.

"You know you want to!" Alyssa commented.

Ashington placed her phone beside her while still recording the moment. "You're already my damn sister-in-law! You might as well

125

make it official!"

"C'mon, Rie." Erykah tilted her head with a sideways smirk on her face. "Hell, we all thought that your ass was a figment of his imagination until we met you face to face. This is your fairytale ending. I was almost stuck with two others. Your ass better say yes."

Cherie turned to Shane, finally, yet the tears came harder and she almost hyperventilated at the ring that Shane showed to her inside the black velvet box that he held in his hand. Shane truly honored the light of his life with the dazzling diamond ring. Created in fourteen-karat rose gold, the engagement ring featured a quarter karat, round diamond center stone. A double squared frame of smaller, round accent diamonds surrounded the center stone while twisting diamond-lined ribbons created the ring's shank. It was no wonder she couldn't breathe.

"Babe, my knee is kind of hurting down here," Shane joked. "Do I have a yes?"

"Leave me alone," she whined as she swatted at him. "I have to get myself together."

Shane shrugged and rose from the floor while closing the box. "If you don't want it then—"

"Stop!" Cherie pouted as she shook her hand with gaped fingers. "You know I want it. Yes, I'll marry you!"

"That's what I thought."

"Don't make fun of me."

With a beaming smile, Shane reopened the box, took the ring out, and then gently slid it onto her finger. "You have no idea how long

I've been waiting to do this. This ain't no Home Economics project, either."

Cherie stood on the tips of her heels despite the fact that she was still nowhere near his dominant height. He curved his arms around her waist as he connected their lips, paying no attention to the salty tears that splashed her lip-gloss. Finally, he had his Rie, and his Rie had her Shane. The moment couldn't have been grander.

"Yo! Y'all need to stop all that shit before Rie ends up pregnant for real!" Ashington commented. "Speaking of which, when are we going to get some nieces and nephews out of her?"

Shane and Cherie broke their kiss when hearing her question. He looked down at his love through bedroom eyes. "Give us about nine months after our wedding. So, I'll say a year from now."

"A year?" Cherie squealed. "Am I not counting right? Shane, you're giving me three months to put together a whole fucking wedding?"

"Three… give or take."

"Have I said that I love you today?"

"No. You've been busy being mad."

Cherie snarled, even though she settled on giving Shane a kiss on the lips.

———

Mandy, almost in tears, burst through the doors of Infusion and stopped on the street. She was breathing all too heavy to be able to catch them. On a whim, she pulled her phone from her clutch and dialed the only number that belonged to the single person that would be willing to hear her.

"Hello?" Davetta answered.

"She's getting married!" she screamed as the tears ran down her face.

"Who, baby?"

"*Cherie*, Auntie! Shane just proposed!"

"He what?"

"She happily accepted, too. Can you believe this?"

"Amanda, don't you think you're a little too old to be jealous of your cousin?"

"It's not fair!" she cried as she stomped her foot. "She knew that I wanted him first!"

"Honey, I don't see what you see in him. You should just stick to Richard like we talked about. He's less crazy, he makes decent money, and he's very laid back—"

"I wanted De'Shane! She just had to hook her fucking claws into him! You would've thought that me not passing messages would've done the fucking trick. Oh no. Here came Jessica, then fucking April, and now *this*!"

"Amanda, let it go."

"Why couldn't you just keep her the fuck away? Why did she have to come back? I was going to make my move, whether it was going through Rich or crying on Shane's fucking shoulder! This is not right!"

"What did you just say?"

The voice she heard was not of Davetta's. Mandy slowly turned around with wide eyes to see, not only her cousin standing there, but Shane and Erykah, who were coming to check on her.

Cherie tilted her head as she approached her cousin. "I asked you what you said, Amanda."

Mandy stood there, merely shivering as her eyes diverted to Shane's.

Eight years ago...

Rich had dapped Shane up and mushed Mandy's head to the side before he left Patricia's to chase yet another skirt. It was a Thursday. One that Apollo had given Shane off for a change. He figured that his son had had enough of working and traveling, so why not let him hang loose a little after school? Patricia had gone off to her second job, leaving the trio alone for the night. Shane remained on the floor of the living room when the house phone rang. He didn't even care to watch Mandy hop up off the couch or enter the kitchen to fetch it.

She pulled her long cornrows behind her back and unlatched the phone from the base. "Anton residence," she answered.

"Hey, cousin," Cherie greeted her lazily.

Mandy leaned back a little and stared at Shane who was mindlessly texting on his two-way pager. She took a little time to admire his royal blue racecar jacket that had the Kellogg's Frosted Flakes logos all over the sleeves, chest, and back. Then, she traveled deeper into the kitchen until she reached the back door where she exited and took her cousin's call on the back porch.

"Mandy?"

"Yea, I'm here," she lightly giggled. "Umm… what's up, cousin?"

"In pain. This sucks."

"It does. But what would you have wanted? To be pregnant by your mom's boyfriend? Think about it. That would've ruined your life and you know it."

"Do you ever really wonder what would've happened if I somehow stayed home?"

"Sometimes." Mandy sighed.

"Right now, I'm wondering what would've happened had I not let Davetta take me to that clinic. It was my baby, Mandy. I don't care how it got here. I would've been a hell of a lot better at being a mother than Davetta. That's for damn sure."

"Don't think like that. Just know that there is something better out there for you."

"You sound so generic right now."

"Well, it's true."

"How's home?" Cherie decided to change the subject so that she wouldn't get too emotional. "Specifically, how is everybody?"

"Or do you mean, *specifically*, how is Shane?"

"You know." Cherie yawned as a side effect of her pain killers. She had taken one more than she was allowed to.

"Shane is Shane. You know it's not my place to tell his business."

"Come on, cousin. You're the only way I have to get close enough to him. Has he asked about me?"

"Rie… unfortunately not."

She could feel the pang in her heart when listening to that answer. How could he not have asked about her? She thought of him every day.

"He's working and what not. What can I say?"

"We're moving again soon," Cherie sadly informed her.

"Yea? Where to?"

"Davetta wants to go further out west. We're going out to California. I don't know where exactly, but that's where we're going. She's been talking to some woman and a guy. I don't know which one we're going to be staying with next, but I know they're loaded."

"You really have the life, you know that?"

"Please. Me constantly moving and trying to avoid hands and eyes on me is not the life."

"You get to see the country and meet new people. You get name brands and big houses—"

"And this is where I'm going to have to stop you and get off the phone. What you think may be heaven is hell for me, Amanda, and I can't sit on the phone with you while you're completely delusional. Tell Aunt Pat to call me."

Mandy heard the dial-tone and pulled the cordless phone away from her ear. She rolled her eyes at it, then went back into the house to place it on the charger. In front of her, bent over inside the refrigerator, was Shane. He had come out of his jacket and was now standing there in a pair of dark blue Levi's, royal blue and white Jordan's, and a white t-shirt. As soon as he closed the fridge and turned around, he could see the lust in Mandy's eyes. He furrowed his brows at the look on her face and slowly approached her.

"Who was on the phone?" he asked.

"No one," she lied.

"Had to be someone. You were out there for almost three minutes."

"Just some guy." As a habit, Mandy fingered one of her braids over her shoulder and wrapped the end around her finger. "A friend gave him my number as a joke."

"Really?"

"Really. So, umm—"

"Have you heard from Rie, lately?"

"No," she lied right off. "That aunt of mine has her moving from place to place, so it's hard to keep up with her, you know."

Shane's head slowly dropped until he was staring at the toes of his newly bought sneakers. "Do you... do you ever think that she's thinking of me?"

"Maybe." She shrugged. "It's been so long. Who knows?"

Shane ran his hand over his thinly trimmed mustache, then awkwardly rubbed the back of his neck. "It would be a shame if she didn't. I think of her more than I should be."

"It's been four years. Don't you think it's time to let it go?"

His head popped up then, and his glare was stronger than it used to be. "What?"

Suddenly, Mandy left the kitchen counter that she was posted against and rushed to Shane. She stood on the tips of her toes to try and peck his lips, yet he dodged it and backed away from her.

"What the fuck are you doing?" he harshly asked. "Are you insane? Girl, what's wrong with you?"

"I thought that—"

"Thought what? That I was your friend, but I would be willing to go there with you? That I would go behind my homie's back and get at you? Or better yet, that I would actually betray your cousin by doing something with you?"

"Shane, we—"

"As far as I'm concerned, this shit never happened. You hear me, Mandy? Don't you ever bring this shit up to anybody. *Anybody.*" Shane left the kitchen, grabbed his pager off of the coffee table, and headed to the door.

"Shane!" Mandy chased after him until he was at the front door.

He turned and snarled at her. "I won't be coming back over here. And don't expect for me to speak to you until you're in your right damn mind."

When Shane left, she was standing there with a shattered and confused heart. If she had it her way, she would blame Rich for leaving her and Shane alone so much to actually grow an attraction to him in the first place. But it wasn't his fault. Mandy had to be honest with herself and admit that she had the hots for Shane since they were ten, when she was first introduced to him by her own cousin.

CHAPTER ELEVEN

Dangerous

"Answer me!" Cherie screamed at Mandy.

"Nah, Rie," Erykah said as she threw her arm in front of her with her eyes hard on Mandy. "You heard what the fuck she said. The bitch just admitted to whomever on the phone that she wanted my brother; your man. She just said, to whom I'm assuming is your mama, that she wanted her to keep you away. Now, this bitch got three seconds to explain herself."

"Cherie—" Mandy couldn't get her statement out with how quickly Cherie stepped forward, grabbed a fistful of her cousin's hair and slammed her face first onto the ground.

She wasn't trying to hear anything that her cousin had to say. Mandy underestimated Cherie and wasn't quite aware of how often she did have to fight others in school because of her beauty threatening the livelihood of other's relationships. She sat on Mandy's shoulders, holding her down by the back of the neck with one hand, and punching her in the back of the head with the other.

Shane wrestled with Erykah to get her away from him so that he could pull Cherie off of Mandy. Getting fed up with his sister blocking his path, he politely picked her up and sat her aside so that he could get to his woman. Successfully, he yanked Cherie off of Mandy and settled her on the soles of her heels.

Cherie wasn't listening to his yelling about how she had to conduct herself. She made sure that she didn't have a hair out of place and straightened her tiara. "And I'm still pretty, bitch!" she spat. "Be jealous of *that!*"

Mandy, with a bleeding mouth and one banging headache, slowly picked herself up off the ground, all the while crying.

Erykah folded her arms and waited for whatever Mandy had to say if anything. Besides her, Quita, Alyssa, and drunken Ashington came out of the doors of the club to see what could've been the matter. They had a bad feeling when Erykah, Shane, and Cherie hadn't returned with Mandy. The trio was in agreeance that there was a possibility that Mandy only left because it was the second proposal within a two-month span, and it wasn't to her.

"What the fuck is wrong with you?" Shane asked her, trying his best to block Cherie in case she had another urge to lunge for her cousin. "Why would you admit some shit like that? You can't be happy for your cousin?"

Mandy's heart broke more than what it was supposed to in that moment. Shane was again defending Cherie. Out of all the years that she had known him, not once had he decided to take up for her or make her life a little easier. She was bleeding for crying out loud, and he didn't even care to come and check her face or the back of her head from the blows she received.

To make matters worse, a white Monte Carlo pulled up to the meter behind Cherie. Rich killed the engine and stepped out with his keys in his hands. As requested, he wore all white with his silver accessories. He had to adjust the small, silver rectangular specs on his face to try and figure out why the group was standing out front, Mandy was disheveled, Erykah looked like she was four seconds away from pouncing, and Cherie was in a fight stance behind Shane in six-inch heels. The closer he got, he recognized the complexity that was his best friend's face.

"What...? What's going on?" he asked nervously, taking a stance next to Shane. "Did I miss the proposal?" He didn't receive an answer. Silence draped the bunch, and it only made his heart pound a little faster. He had already gathered that Mandy had gotten her ass beat, but by who, he hadn't known. Everyone else was still primped. "Mandy—"

"Cherie attacked me!" she wailed.

Cherie tried to push Shane out of her way, but he wrapped his arm around her waist to restrain her.

Mandy flinched and took a step back. She was caught in a very bad position, seeing as how she knew Erykah from school, and she knew that Erykah Cruz was always ready to throw down. Then, there was the fact that Alyssa was standing a little too close to her. She was deathly in arm's length in case Alyssa wanted to reach out and touch her.

"You're goddamn right I attacked you, bitch!" Cherie spat from

137

around Shane's arm. "Can you get out of my way?"

"No!" Shane yelled at her. "You're not going to jail when we just got engaged. It ain't happening!"

"She just stood there and wished bad on me to my own mama, and then confessed to wanting you!"

The sisters stood in shock at what they had missed.

"Wait." Rich stepped back and took off his glasses. "What?"

Shane took the reins to keep Cherie from getting even more heated. "Mandy got her wires crossed or something because she just told Davetta that she should've kept Cherie away, and then told her that she wanted me."

"My bro?" Rich asked Mandy.

Alyssa dropped her folded arms as she stepped out of her black, double platform snakeskin stilettos. "You mean to tell me that not only did you fuck my nigga, but you're after my brother, too?"

Rich quickly walked up to his woman to try and keep her from doing any more damage.

"You're one fucked up bitch in the head!"

"Baby, calm down," Rich said lowly.

"Ain't no motherfuckin' calmin' down. Cherie had every right to maul this jealous ass bitch! Did you think that you were gonna get a chance to fuck both of 'em? This bitch might have VD! Rich, your ass is going to get tested on Monday morning, and so am I! Get your damn hands off me!" She pulled her arms away from his grasp as she tried to walk around him, but he wasn't letting her go anywhere.

"Why are you all trying to attack me when Shane is just as guilty as I am!" Mandy screamed.

Shane's head whipped around to her with his brow cocked. "And what the fuck is Shane guilty of, exactly?"

"The day we kissed—"

"No, you mean the day you *tried* to kiss me! Don't you ever get that shit twisted. I stepped away from you and asked you what the fuck was wrong with you! You asked me to let the memory of your cousin go, then I left Ms. Pat's house and never came back, as I had promised you. Don't try to stand there and act like I participated in some shit. Everybody out here knows that I'm a horrible ass liar, so they know I ain't lyin' when I say that I never kissed your ass."

While speaking, Cherie had her back to him as she paced. Shane should've had eyes in the back of his head. Had he had them, he would've seen it when Cherie peeled off her heels, neatly placed her tiara on the hood of the Monte Carlo that Rich borrowed from Shane, and removed her sheer covering, leaving on the black fashionable bra and high-waist bottoms. As soon as she turned around, at the end of Shane's sentence, she ran around him and pushed herself off the ball of her left foot just to Superman Punch the hell out of Mandy. Cherie hadn't thought of her fresh manicure. She couldn't even feel it when two of her nails broke. She one-two punched Mandy's face systematically and quickly. This time, it took a little more time for Shane to get her off her cousin.

"She deserves that ass whippin'!" Alyssa yelled around Rich's arm.

"Damn," Quita commented on the sidelines. "I didn't know Rie had it in her."

Erykah placed her hand on her hip. "She ain't a weak bitch, that's for damn sure. Looks like I ain't got to come up out of earrings and heels for her."

Ashington propped herself up on Quita's shoulder by her forearm and lazily pointed at Shane struggling to balance Cherie as she kicked her naked feet in the air while they backed away. "Am I that fucked up to where I heard that Rich's ex said, in front of his fiancée, that she wanted her cousin, our sister-in-law's man, who just happens to be our brother?"

"Ash... shut the fuck up."

Shane propped Cherie against the Monte Carlo, but she wasn't done speaking her peace. "You see the size of this fuckin' rock?" Cherie yelled. "It ain't about the fuckin' money, you dumb hoe! This is experience! This is work! This is hurt and happiness all wrapped into one! I earned this shit! I didn't have to chase after someone else's man to get it! And this most definitely ain't about you, you stupid bitch! Gonna smile in my face and wish bad on me? I should molly-whop the fuck out of your ass again! Just knock some goddamn sense into you!"

"Why did it have to always be about you?" Mandy cried. Her words were almost inaudible.

"You made it about me, bitch! I've been through too much shit for somebody to try and come behind me to take what I've worked for, whether it's money, material shit, or my motherfuckin' man!"

"Why do you have to get everything?"

"I *didn't* have everything! You only *thought* I did, but you never stopped to see what I went through for all that shit! I didn't ask for none of it!"

"Hold on, hold on." Erykah stepped in. She approached the center of the two women who were adjacent to one another. "Now this shit is just now hittin' me, and correct me if I'm wrong because what I'm thinking makes perfectly good sense." On the balls of her heels, she turned to her brother and narrowed her eyes. "Did you or did you not tell me that you asked Mandy about Cherie very often?"

"Yea," he replied. "But what that got to do with anything?"

"And did you or did you not receive the answer of her not speaking to her cousin, so you gave up hope?"

"Yea."

"Uh-huh. And Rie... in one of our conversations, when we were still getting the feel for one another... did you or did you not tell me that you would ask Mandy about Shane, but she would tell you that it wasn't her place to tell you what was going on?"

"You're damn skippy," Cherie responded angrily.

"Now, we're here, scrappin' like a motherfucker when the confession comes out that this bitch wanted my brother. Does it hit anybody else that her excuse of not wanting to be messy and tell y'alls business to each other is bullshit? Does it make sense that she was withholding messages to keep y'all apart?"

"You motherfuckin' hoe!" Alyssa screamed.

By now, the gatherers had started to spill out of Infusion and onto the curb. Erykah didn't care. She grabbed the back of Rich's black polo, yanking him off her sister to set her free. Like a wild animal, Alyssa took a running start for Mandy who had struggled to get on her feet. The blow that Alyssa sent to her jaw knocked her off her feet and sent her flying out of her heels.

Alyssa stumbled before she caught her balance. "You just a manipulative bitch, huh?"

Mandy tried her best to weakly fight back, but it wasn't doing much.

Quita and Erykah were pushing and pulling Rich to keep him away from Alyssa. They were arguing with him over why they wouldn't let him go. The spectators, however, were wondering what the hell was going on.

"You tried it!" Cherie yelled around Shane's arms while he tried his best to keep her from getting off the hood of the car. "This here is real love! We still came together!"

Mandy had somehow gotten on top of Alyssa and grabbed a handful of her hair. That's all she could do with what little strength she had. Neither of them realized that their designer cocktail dress had rolled up and was exposing their thongs. The street woman that was Alyssa meant the pain of her scalp hadn't fazed her. It wasn't the first time that she had gotten into a brawl or a catfight. She wrapped her hands around Mandy's throat and forced her on her back. Alyssa bitch-slapped Mandy while still having her natural hair pulled, threatening to be ripped out of her scalp.

One of the clients who showed up to the event decided to step in and pull Alyssa off.

Shane threw Cherie over his shoulder so that he could carry her to his car. "Quita!" he called over the opposite shoulder. "Get Rie's stuff, and thank the management and whatever. Y'all control this shit!"

Quita obliged as she finally let go of Rich. Erykah looked down at Mandy on the ground and shook her head. The girl had what was coming to her.

Ashington stumbled over to Mandy and whacked her with her clutch. "You know you're wrong. Shame on you," she said with a hiss.

"Rich, you help that bitch up and walk her to her car," Alyssa spat while running her fingers through her naturally long and wavy tresses.

"She doesn't have one," he replied, out of breath.

"Then take her motherfuckin' ass home. On the way there, you explain to this bitch why she's exiled, because I'm pretty sure that her delusional ass doesn't understand just yet."

"Baby—"

"Richard, be a gentleman. We have to stay here and clean up after our sister-in-law's party. She got what was comin' to her, and now, send her ass back home, hell. Either that or else I pounce on that ass again for eyeballin' the shit out of me earlier. Oh, and let her know that, if she thinks of pressin' charges, that me or my sisters will be comin' for her manipulative ass."

Rich shook his head at how his fiancée spoke as if Mandy wasn't sitting on the ground with her hair all over the place and her strapless, white dress newly designed with blood droplets. "Come on, Amanda," he dryly said to her.

"I don't need your help," she barked as she picked herself up off the concrete slab. Mandy took her time to find her shoes and her phone, and then located her Uber app through her cracked screen. She limply strolled down the block away from Infusion, angry, hurt, and emotionally overwhelmed.

Cherry and royal blue lights sped down the street toward her. The sight of them caused her eyes to bulge. She wanted badly to flag them down for help but thought better of it. The family rushed Alyssa inside Infusion so that she wouldn't be hauled off to jail. One car stopped in front of Mandy, blocking her path.

A tall, brown skinned cop hopped out of his cruiser and approached her with worry etched onto his face. "Ma'am, what happened here?" he asked her. "Who attacked you?"

Mandy gulped when thinking of Alyssa's words. "A girl I didn't know," she answered. "She came to my cousin's birthday party and words were thrown. She attacked me first, and then her friends jumped in. They sped off, officer."

"Did you happen to catch her first and last name?"

"I didn't. My cousin might know, but her fiancé whisked her away because she was trying to defend me, and he didn't want her to get arrested for assault."

"And they just left you here?"

"I guess they weren't thinking." She shrugged.

"Stay right here for me, okay? Don't move." The officer left her in the backseat of his cruiser so that he could link up with his brothers in blue to get a straight story of what actually happened.

With a new set of tears erupting, she went to her texts to send her aunt a message of what had happened since Davetta had obviously hung up. There, she saw the message Davetta sent after hanging up.

"I'm calling the police on these savage ass animals!"

CHAPTER TWELVE

Never Really Mattered

Cherie burst through the doors of the home first and started to jet up the stairs when Joyce called for her from the dining room. Cherie's trail was bent in the way that she had to go to her honorary mother's call. Shane slowly followed behind his angry woman with her heels and her covering in his hands.

"What's the matter with your face, Rie?" Joyce asked as she stood from the seat where she sat. "Honey, it's your birthday. You're not supposed to look so upset."

Cherie slapped her hands down on her bare thighs before she could explain. "The Lord knows that when I woke up this morning, it was not my intention to end up fighting, period, let alone fighting my own cousin, Mama J."

Joyce's face scrunched. "Fight your cousin?"

"And… *this* fool…" She tilted her head while blindly pointing her fingers at Shane in the entryway of the dining room. "He pissed me off this morning, got me on the verge of tears because I'm thinking he's missing my special day... but then he pops up, proposes to me, makes everything better, and I'm lighter than a feather and all in love and shit. I noticed my cousin is missing the moment. So, me, Shane, and Erykah go to check on her. We walk out of the club to overhear her conversation with my mama, Mama J! Apparently, she's been wanting Shane. Erykah busted it wide open that Mandy was holding messages away from us just to keep us apart."

"Why would she do that?"

"Because she's been wanting him!"

"Ma—" Shane began, but Cherie cut him off.

"And *you*? You never told me that she tried to kiss you, Shane. I mean, what the fuck?"

"Does it matter now?"

"Yes, it fucking matters now! She tried to kiss you!"

"To be honest with you, I almost forgot about it. I was mad and avoided her altogether after that. The only time me and her were in a room together after that was when Ms. Pat passed. By then, I had gone through so much that I forgot. Then you come home and made me remember that I was still missing you, so I jumped into action with trying to make you happy. Baby, you can't fault me for that."

"You know what?" Cherie pulled in a breath, emphasizing it with her hands. Then, she let it go with her eyes closed tight. She was truly trying to calm herself. "You know what's more important to me right now, De'Shane?"

"What, babe?"

"The fact that you only gave me three months to put this wedding together. I will not even begin to think of nothing else other than the fact that this negro gave me a short amount of time to pull in everything that will make our happy ending, *happy*. I need to choose a date, run it by you, choose dresses, a location… I don't have time for bullshit. Oh, and I have my convention next weekend with Erykah. So, what Cherie is going to do is focus on *happy*." With that, she went up to the master bedroom to remove her clothing.

Shortly after, Shane entered and placed her shoes in the closet. Then, he stripped down to his underwear and went to the bed where his love was sending a text message to Erykah, letting her know that she was home and that everything was okay.

"Still mad?" Shane asked her.

"What are you going to do about school?" she countered.

"I'll have to re-register all over again, why?"

"We once had goals, Shane. You mentioned Home Economics, and it reminded me of our decisions. You were supposed to graduate. Your major wasn't even Architectural Design. So, what are we going to do?"

"Baby, can you stop doing that? You quickly move on to the next subject to avoid the topic at hand. But you know what I'm going to do?" Shane crawled into bed and slipped her phone from her fingers with ease. With soft lips, he gently kissed Cherie close to her ear and whispered. "I'm going to stop knowing everything about you, and I'm just going to go with the flow."

A small smile donned her face. "Thank you," she blushed. "Now, what are you we going to do about the wedding versus our career moves and education?"

"Well, I'll re-register at the end of November to make sure that I get in for the second semester. Hopefully, they won't make me repeat an entire year, but that's for better wishing. We're still going to marry no matter what. It's too late to change my major. With what I obtain, I'll run the restaurant and hand over the other business to Rich and Lyssa. Then, I'll put you through school, if need be. In the meantime..." Shane grabbed one of Cherie's legs and pulled it over to the other side of him, to adjust himself perfectly at her center. "I think we have to start trying for that baby again."

Passionately, they kissed and proceeded to commemorate their engagement. Fairytale come true? *Almost.*

Cherie strutted through the ballroom of the grand hotel where she would be staying for the weekend. Erykah promised to meet her there after she had the nap that she was dying for. Ahead of her was a thick, young woman, classily dressed in a black pantsuit that hugged her every curve. As expected, she was off to herself, scanning the room to find a familiar face. Cherie snuck up on her with a smile and tapped April on the shoulder.

When April registered Cherie, she threw a surprised and relieved smile onto her face as she spread her arms.

"Girl, you look good!" Cherie complimented her as she embraced April.

"Why thank you, diva." April pulled away and stretched her leg so that Cherie could see her heels of choice.

"Jealousy! All over my face!"

April's heels were black crushed velvet. They were double platform pumps with a skinny heel on them and had a strap across the ankle. The topping on the cake was the gold chains that fastened at the heel and crossed the stiletto.

"I saw them and had to have them," April said. "I thought that you might like them. Hell, I almost didn't come to this event, but Erykah insisted and Rodney told me that he would come since he was looking for his next business venture."

"Rodney?" Cherie asked with a contorted face until she remembered having a helping hand in pulling the two together. Her features softened as her smile returned. "That's right! How are you guys?"

"I have to really thank you and Erykah, Cherie. Rodney is not only a breath of fresh air, but he has no emotional ties to his ex. We've been happy since our very first conversation. He's a really great man. At first, I thought that we were moving too quickly, but it just feels right, you know?"

"I know what you mean."

"You and Shane? How are you two? Better I hope."

"Your sacrifice didn't go in vain." Cherie lifted her left hand to show the ring that Shane had Erykah to take her time and craft after hours.

"This is beautiful!" April gushed with Cherie's hand held gently inside of her own. "I'm so happy for you guys! It seems that love really does prevail."

"It does."

"Mon Cherie?"

She turned her head just in time to see Rodney walk up beside her. His five-eleven height seemed inferior to her six-one in her pumps. She hugged him from the side as to not make it any more awkward than it had to be. "How are you, Rod?" she asked him with a beaming smile. "You got you a good woman over here. I see you've upgraded."

"With your help, of course." Rodney chuckled just before giving April a loving kiss on the cheek. He wrapped one arm around her waist. Something that she loved since her ex and her family would always remind her of how seemingly big she was. "I always told Terry that you had good taste, Cherie. You bringing this beautiful and artistic woman into my life was proof of that."

April blushed with her head hanging to hide it.

"Girl! Look at that suit!" Erykah cheered as she approached. She didn't care for the snooty people in the room who turned to look at her. She would always be her usual loud and ghetto self before pretending to be someone she wasn't for the approval of people she didn't know or like. When she was close enough, she stretched her arms out and flexed her fingers to call for April's hands. "You lookin' good, April! I don't have my phone or else I would have to take a selfie."

"Here," Cherie offered. "Take my phone." Out of her blazer, Cherie pulled her cell phone from her pocket. Oddly enough, Shane had yet to text her since she boarded her flight six hours prior. It wasn't like him to go without speaking to her unless he was up to something. She smirked as she handed her phone over to Erykah.

"What?" Erykah asked as a very suspicious feel overtook her.

"Your brother thinks he's slick, but I know him better now."

"What do you mean?"

"He hasn't hit me since I boarded. I wouldn't be surprised if his sneaky self is in my room when I get back upstairs."

Erykah rolled her eyes as the group got into position to take one good-looking selfie that would be posted on all of their Instagram accounts along with the hashtag "RoyalSixxFamily".

After an event of meeting people, knocking back a few drinks, and mingling with people that they either already knew or had met online, the women were ready to retire to their suites. April had to give the girls one last hug before going up to her room with her man, leaving Erykah and Cherie to catch an elevator on their own.

"She looks happy as hell," Erykah said after the doors closed.

"She does. I'm happy for her. Now I can officially stop feeling guilty about ruining her wedding."

"You shouldn't have felt bad in the first place. They had a choice of what they were going to do with their lives. I put money on the fact that they were going to get an annulment shortly after."

"That's not nice," Cherie said with a giggle.

"Well, it's true. Have you heard from troublesome Terry?"

"Hell naw. I like it that way. The next time he steps to me, I won't be able to stop Shane from taking his life, and I'm not going to try either."

"Davetta?"

"She texted me yesterday asking me why I had yet to tell her that I was engaged."

"Like she gives a fuck."

"Really."

"Oh, I spotted the perfect gothic church for you during our flight. I'll call in the morning to check for pricing. Cherie, it looks just like a castle."

"Really?" she gushed.

"Swear you and Shane were meant for each other. Y'all are so dramatic, precise, and over the top."

"Leave us alone," she giggled.

When the elevator dinged, they stepped off and gave each other hugs, then parted ways.

Cherie, forgetting all about the suspect behavior of her fiancé, swiped her key card and stepped into the room. Hearing the door close behind her, she climbed out of her heels and blazer, leaving them both near the front door. On her way to the room, she remembered that she left her phone in her blazer pocket. With haste, she retrieved it and scurried into her room, ready to dive into her bed. If Cherie's halt had sound effects, it would've sounded like screeching tires when her feet skipped across the carpet.

Her eyes fell upon a fit god with a V-shaped cut in his hips that dipped behind the shoulders of a fluffy teddy bear that he held in front of his manhood. Shane stared at her through bedroom eyes as he seductively licked his thick lips. His dreads hung freely over his shoulders, and it made Cherie confused as to whether to go over and pull them first or move the bear out of the way to grab his rod.

"Surprise," he said in a baritone that shouldn't have been allowed since it spoke to Cherie's loins.

"What… what are you…?" She stopped speaking only to scratch at her short, curled hair. "Baby… what you doin' here?"

"I think I was shooting blanks last week. You're off your period now. I think it's the perfect time to try that again."

"We're going to overlook the way you just grossed me out. Bring all of that over here."

"Nah. I think you should come and get your gift… along with something else."

Without another word to spare, Cherie narrowed her lids and strolled over to him with so much boldness that she almost scared herself. She snatched the bear out of his hands and tossed it onto the bed along with her cell phone.

Shane, however, always had to outdo her with the dramatics. He spun her around, lifted her skirt, and then ripped a hole inside her stockings. Aggressively, he pulled her panties aside. He proclaimed, "This is going to hurt… *a lot.*"

Half the floor could hear the howl that Cherie let out at Shane's invasion. Within another thirty minutes, they were on a half-naked bed, sweaty, and hardly being able to breathe. Shane had one of Cherie's legs over his shoulders. The only thing that he allowed her to keep on was her jewelry and her heels. He tried to readjust them to where she would land on top of him, yet he miscalculated how far to the edge of the bed that they had already been. The two landed on the floor with him still inside of her.

Cherie, still as bold as ever, decided that she could reverse-cowgirl on Shane to make him cum quicker, but he took advantage of it. Full advantage. With his back against the side of the bed, he had more leverage. He scooped his arms underneath the bends of her legs and locked his fingers behind her back.

"Did I say that you could take control yet?" he asked her.

"Shane—"

"Fuck that. We ain't been able to get as nasty as we've wanted to because we're always worried about waking Miracle."

"Baby—" Cherie tried to close her legs, yet Shane's elbows were preventing that from happening. He had her as wide open as she could be. Cherie knew that there was nothing but pain and pleasure that was about to take place when Shane planted his feet firmly on the floor.

"I want you to sound off," he told her.

As if his dick was a real drill, he pounded Cherie from underneath. She couldn't catch her breath for the life of her. Her head tilted back to rest on Shane's shoulder, leaving her neck exposed to his ever so sensual kisses. Before she knew it, a familiar feeling had surfaced. Not just any feeling.

"Shane!" she cried.

"Let it go," he whispered.

As soon as he pulled out of her, Cherie's stomach collapsed as her body convulsed. Shane had made her squirt all over the rug on the side of the bed. She couldn't feel bad about it since technically it wasn't her fault.

Her whimpers were like music to his ears. Violently, he shoved himself back inside of her to repeat the waterfall that he knew was coming and hard.

"Baby!" she chorused.

"Fuck that. How bad you want this baby, Rie?"

She couldn't answer. Her words were stuck and her eyes were rolling inside of her skull. He had her in that distant place that Terry and Damon could never get her to. While Damon was close, he didn't know how to pull the strings. He damn sure couldn't make Cherie feel like a woman. There was no way, even with an instructions manual, could he make her release glad water like Shane could.

"You done?" he whispered as he kept his pace.

"No," she whined.

"You sure?"

"No!"

Shane unwrapped his arms to make Cherie bounce on her own. Once she created a steady rhythm, mixing the whip of her hips every now and again, Shane reached around her and slapped her pussy. At first, it hurt, but she liked it. Three more slaps and he had her basically twerking on his dick. She was only moving her wiggling ass over the head of his pole. It was a tease, but she considered it payback for the torture and pleasure. She looked down to see that she had Shane's toes curling. Cherie knew that Shane was chewing his bottom lip off by now, which was why he remained quiet.

"Where did all that shit talking go, baby?" she asked him between heavy breaths.

"Fuck," he grunted. "You gon' do me like this?"

"Hell yea. Cum for me, daddy."

"Don't do that," he said through a strained breath. Shane's head rolled back on his shoulders. His eyes were squeezing so tightly that his lashes were damn near touching his iris.

"Do what? I'm just giving you what you want."

"You know I love it when you call me that."

"When I call you what? Daddy?"

"Stop," he managed through closed teeth.

Purposely, Cherie removed her hands from her knees and leaned forward. Her knees hit the carpeted floor along with her hands and breasts. The only thing left in the air was her wiggling backside. "Look at it, daddy," she cooed.

"No."

Harder, she twerked to make him open his eyes. He grabbed onto her cheeks as if trying to stop them. He wasn't ready to stop. Unfortunately, Cherie slapped his hands out of the way and clenched her walls tighter around him.

"Give me what I want," she told him seriously. "You give it to me or I'll take it."

"Baby…" Whatever he was about to say was overshadowed by the rise of the climax he was desperately fighting.

Cherie leaned forward just a little more so that he could see the action a little clearer and only clapped her cheeks. Her orgasm was right in front of her, but her intentions were to get him off first.

She knew she had him when he reached down and grabbed as much of her short-cut as he could, and tugged a little. Underneath her, his legs trembled. His knees locked.

"Fuck!" he called to the walls. "Shit, you cheated."

Cherie couldn't stop. Her pussy swallowed the rest of his shaft and her hips swung wildly.

"Baby!" Shane gripped her hips. His toes were popping with how hard he was trying to hold on to another orgasm approaching at full speed. "Cherie!"

"Call me, daddy," she moaned. "Say my name one more time."

"Cherie, baby, damn!"

Her head tossed back. The lovers felt the vibrations of one another's bodies. It was always something about the majestic moment of arriving at the same time. It was something that they would never get tired of.

Once their breaths calmed a little, Cherie rested her cheek against Shane's rising and falling, sweaty chest.

"Get the fuck off me, Cherie," he demanded.

"No," she giggled.

"Get your ass up."

"Why?"

"Because you weren't supposed to rape me like that."

"*Rape?*" she squealed, looking up at him. "Who raped who, Shane?"

"I came over here as a Christian. Hopped a whole jet to get here by the time you had already landed. I thought that I was getting me a wholesome girl, you wicked city woman."

"Shut up," she laughed.

"You took advantage of me, Cherie. That's not okay."

"Whatever. You can't rape the willing."

"How the fuck do we get off the floor?" he asked, changing the subject.

"Can we stay here for a little bit?" Cherie grumbled. "My knees and my back hurt. I don't think I'll be able to move. You didn't let me stretch before basically making me a goddamn pretzel on that bed."

"I'm sorry," he tiredly chuckled. "We can stay here for a little bit. But then… we're going to have to crawl to the shower. We're all sticky and shit."

"We are. You think we succeeded?"

"With the baby?"

"Yea. Like… what if we didn't? What if—"

"Cherie. Shut up. We gon' make it do what it do, at all cost."

"But, Shane—"

"I love you, baby."

"I love you, too," she sighed. Deep down, Cherie was afraid that lightening wouldn't strike three times in the same place. With what little hope she had, she dozed off before they could get into the shower. Like when they were children, she trusted Shane, and that's all she could do.

CHAPTER THIRTEEN

Sign Of The Times

A whole month and a few weeks had passed, and fortunately, everything was falling into place. Cherie was ready to scout the location of her new store before she could open it, but Erykah let her know that she could sell online as long as she needed to and import her own jewels to have them sent to the Royal Sixx's. The three women were getting along under one roof whenever all three were actually at the store, and things in everyone's lives seemed to be perfect.

On this particular morning, Cherie awoke to a kiss on her sideburn. Her lips stretched into a smile. Then, something warm accompanied by heavy breaths touched her cheek. Saliva slid over the bridge of her nose, yet it didn't take away her smile.

"Morning, my *loves*," she tiredly cheered. Her eyes fluttered open and she leaned off her pillows. The first face she saw was Miracle's. Shane had already wrangled her thick locks into two ponytails and dressed her in a pair of jeans, her little red and white Chuck Taylor's, and her red short-sleeved shirt that had a white star on the front. "You're going off to school without me?" Cherie asked her in a raspy voice.

Miracle grabbed both sides of Cherie's face and gave her yet another kiss on the nose.

"Aww, she doesn't want to leave you," Shane lightly chuckled. "C'mon, Ren. Let's let Rie get herself together."

"Babe," Cherie whined. "Are you going to be gone for a while?"

"I got to work, baby." He rose from the bed with Miracle propped up on his arm. When he turned to look at her, he displayed his pearly whites to put her at ease a little.

Cherie admired his red polo with an asymmetrical, white stripe descending from his shoulder to his hip. Per every day, he and Miracle were complementing one another. They both wore their red and white Chuck's for the day. Cherie pouted, seeing that he was fully dressed.

"What's the matter, babe?" Shane asked her. "You want to stay home for the day?"

Sadly, Cherie nodded in response. Her mouth tasted like ash and her stomach was very tight. For the last three or four days, she wasn't able to keep anything down. It wasn't morning sickness. She was afraid that she might've caught a stomach virus. She wouldn't dare tell Shane that she was constipated.

"Alright, my love. How about I give you an assignment?"

"Assignment?" she chorused.

"Look, I'm going to talk to Bo today. I set a reminder a few days ago when I remembered that I was supposed to be doing it awhile ago. I need to get to the bottom of things and decide whether or not to let him go. So... I want you to have a sit down with Davetta before the wedding."

"Shane, I love you. You know I do. I'm not willing to do that for you though."

"Come on, baby. When we have our rehearsal dinner, I don't expect any fuck-ups. We're already in the place that we've been fighting to get to for a while. The last thing that I want to deal with is you either hulking the fuck out or bursting into tears because something isn't right. We have six weeks, Rie. Six whole weeks until we take those vows. You worked hard on your fantasy ceremony, and you've put in too much work in a short amount of time to pull it all together for real. I don't want you uncomfortable after all of this."

"Fine."

"And with Mandy."

"What?" she shrieked.

"We don't need somebody bustin' up in the church when the pastor asks if anybody there doesn't agree with our union. That means the only other person that would disagree would be your boy, Terry. And trust me, baby. I'm lying dead in waiting on him to do it."

"Fine, Shane. Go and take care of your business. I'll hold off on getting my nails done. I'm not about to waste a whole other manicure on either of them."

"Do that." He rounded the foot of the bed to usher yet another kiss before handling his business for the day.

As soon as Cherie heard the alarm activate, she crawled out of bed and went to the bathroom to try and brush her teeth. The taste of ash wasn't a pleasant one. Once her toothbrush reached her molars, her stomach knotted, her throat tightened. Before heading to the toilet, she grabbed a pregnancy test from underneath the sink and opened it. She had to see if her suspicions were true. The only thing that held her back was her thoughts of food poisoning.

The first stick read positive for her pregnancy. The second and third that were also packed inside her box gave her the same result. In a hurry, she called Joyce and Josiah to have them meet her at her clinic. She was going to have to do a walk-in because she wanted to be absolutely sure that this was happening.

In a swanky bungalow that sat off to itself at the edge of a cul-de-sac, Bo pulled the curtain in his living room back to see Shane's white Monte Carlo pull into the driveway. He licked his lips, knowing that this meeting was important. He was going to be open and honest with the boy that he helped to raise.

Shane needn't to knock. He was always welcome inside Bo's home. He entered and took off his shades. To make Bo feel a little easier, he offered up a smile. The two embraced in a tight and manly hug.

"Good to see you," Bo said lowly over Shane's shoulder.

Shane pulled away and took a seat on the black velvet couch in the sitting room. "Let's get to it, fam."

"Get to what, exactly?" Bo went over to the buffet in the far corner and took the crystal top off his jug. "What have I done now?"

"What's up with the trips, the drugs, the women…" Shane looked up at Bo as he was bringing his crystal glass half-filled with brown liquor up to his lips. "...and the liquor?"

Bo took his time to taste the sting of his Jack Daniels as he swirled the rest around in his glass. "I, uh... I have a problem," he admitted. "Apollo was all I had until... well... you know. We all took it hard, and some people cope in different ways. I'm no different. Everybody else can go home to loved ones and *kids*. I come home to absolutely nothing. My best friend, the only man that I've ever trusted, is gone. He was my family. Afterward, it seems like all his kids and his woman overlooked me like I just wasn't there. Even my work was affected. Your little homie made sacrifices for me that I didn't think he would. I mean, I didn't appreciate having to be watched over like some child, but it's what was needed."

"Why didn't you say something, Bo? I thought I kept you comfortable?"

"Shane, you basically fired me, man. Giving me money on top of that doesn't help. Like everybody, I have a stash that I could've lived off of."

"Then tell me what I could've done to make it right."

"You could've been there!" Bo threw his glass inside the fireplace with so much passion that Shane flinched. "Nobody asked me how the fuck I was feelin'! Nobody stopped living their busy lives to check on me, Shane! I lost my family, man! My family. You of all people know what it feels like to lose. So what? What did you think I was? Just some henchman?"

"Nah, Bo. You know I didn't see you like that."

"Then what stopped you?"

"I thought you were okay."

"Well, I *wasn't!*" The end of his sentence was barely audible, but Shane got the point. Bo's hands trembled as his face contorted. He was losing feeling in his body. Bo squatted with his head hanged. "I wasn't alright, man. Everything as I knew it just got shot to hell and fell apart. I don't have my brother here with me no more. I don't have the kids that I considered mine, too. On top of that, I can't work like I used to. I'm a mule now. It don't get no lower than that."

For comfort, Shane got up and went over to his grieving and hurting family. He placed a gentle hand on Bo's back, but something caught his attention within the ashes of the fireplace. A burned glass pipe. Tears gathered in Shane's eyes at the thought of how far Bo had fallen and nobody ever saw it coming. He looked down as Bo grabbed at his own skull, accidently exposing the track marks on his bare arms in various spots on top of poking veins. Harder Shane rubbed his back, trying his best to subside the pain and tears. It made sense as to why Bo always wore long sleeves and blazers.

"Bo," Shane weakly called him. "I know that you love the family, but how much do you love yourself?"

"What?" He swiped his thumb across his nose to get rid of any mucus that may have run out at the time.

"You got to do better. To show you how much this family still loves you, we're going to come with you to receive accelerated detox at—"

"No!" Bo sprung up as he slapped Shane's hand away from him. His eyes were as almost wide as saucers. "I don't have a problem."

Shamefully, Shane mumbled, "There's a crack pipe in the fireplace."

"I had a friend over—"

"And you want to lie to me?" he asked with a hiss. Shane pointed at his own chest. "To me, Bo? You looked at me like I was your son, but you're going to lie to my face? You have motherfuckin' needle marks on your arms, bruh! You don't have a problem? It's nine in the fucking morning and you're drinking, but nah, you don't have a fuckin' problem."

"If you would just listen to what I got to say—"

"Ain't nothin' you can say to me other than the fact that you're going to Coleman!"

Bo's front door came open and Rich stepped through. Unlike Shane, he was dressed in black from head to toe.

"Tell him, Rich!" Bo pleaded. "Tell him how I ain't got no problem!"

Rich looked to Shane as he took off his shades. "I had to tell him about the coke, Bo. I'm sorry, OG."

"You dimed me?"

"Look, you're the closest thing that we have to Apollo and the only father that *some* of us kids ever had. That goes for me. With your foot up my ass about these girls, keepin' myself up, and randomly slidin' me a bill for my grades every now and again, I looked up to you, Bo. In no point in time do I want to look *down* at you."

"I always knew that you were a liar, Rich," Bo managed through closed teeth.

Rich bowed his head as he reached behind him and opened the door a little more. "The boys downtown told me about your experiments. They said that you were shootin' up, but I didn't want to believe. Enough is enough. We lost one father. We can't lose another." Once Rich opened the door as far as it would go, Bo slowly trailed into the atrium to see two buff white men stepping up on his porch. A white van was behind them.

"You motherfucker," he said breathlessly. "You brought motherfuckers from Coleman to my house?"

"It's what's best before you kill yourself."

Bo whirled around to Shane with anger written across his face. "You're going to let this happen?" he roared.

"To get you back?" Shane sadly asked. "To get you healthy again? To get our uncle and father in you again? Yes."

"No," Bo pleaded. He bolted for the hall to grab his gun from the table there, yet he wouldn't be able to make it because the men from the facility grabbed his arms and dragged him out of his home, kicking and screaming obscenities.

Rich went over to Shane and wrapped a single arm around his shoulders. "He'll be alright, man."

Even though it hurt, he would've rather done something while he could, than sit around and let the last piece of his father go.

———

Cherie paced inside the clinic, constantly ringing her hands.

Joyce smiled at her as she patted Josiah's leg.

"Pumpkin, why don't you try to have a seat?" he politely asked her.

"Daddy, I can't," she replied irritably. "It's so many questions, so many—"

"Cherie, you're getting ready to marry Shane, finally," Joyce spoke. "You're getting the wedding of your dreams. You're still young, and you still have eggs, honey. Even if the results come back negative, there will still be plenty of time. Believe me, I know my son. And in knowing him, I'd say that he will stop at nothing to give you what you want."

When the door to the examination room came open, Cherie finally stopped pacing.

"I'm Dr. Heirs," the short Asian woman introduced herself. "Your doctor is on vacation, unfortunately."

"Dr.—"

"You want me to get to the point. I understand." Gently, she closed the door and patted the examination table, prompting Cherie to have a seat. "Well, Ms. Anton, you're pregnant."

"Thank you!" she screamed.

"However…"

"It always has to be a 'however' somewhere in the mix." Cherie rolled her eyes.

"You're only four weeks along. I would like for you to remain on bedrest for the next two months."

"Wait a minute, Dr. Heirs. I can't stay on bedrest. I have a wedding—"

"That your sisters-in-law won't mind keeping you updated with," Joyce interrupted. "And on your wedding day, I'm very sure that your father can walk you nice and slow so that we don't lose this little angel."

Cherie couldn't stop her blush from forming on her face.

"Would you like a sonogram?" Dr. Heirs asked her.

"No!" she blurted. "I don't want to see it until my fiancé gets to see it. I want to enjoy the moment with him."

"We can make an appointment if you'd like, but you have to remain on bedrest. This is a high-risk pregnancy."

The rest of the doctor's words went into one of her ears and out of the other. Nothing else mattered besides the fact that her dreams had finally come true. Even though she knew that Shane based everything off of their school project, it was still a good feeling to know that he cared that much to give her what he felt she deserved.

———————

Shane paced in the living room of his home with his phone pressed against his ear. He was listening closely as the assistant director explained Bo's chaotic intake. He was worried, but he knew that they would be able to get the work done. He had just come from signing off on paperwork and had seen to it that Rich was okay before he had gone to work. Bo put up one hell of a fight during it all until they sedated him.

Through the front door, Cherie spun around with her arms spread wide. The smile on her face made Shane pull his thumb away from his chin and wonder what the hell had gotten into her.

"Well, thank you, Ms. Wright. I appreciate the heads up," he said. "Call me if you have anything else that I should know."

Cherie stopped spinning and looked at his saddened features. "What's wrong, baby?"

"We got Bo admitted into the Coleman today," he sadly said.

"What? Why?"

"Baby, he had a crack pipe at the crib, track marks on his arms, and Rich had already told me that he was snortin' work."

"Bo? Apollo's right hand?"

"Bo, baby."

"I'm so sorry," she sadly sang as she wrapped her arms around his neck.

"It's alright. It was a must."

"I have some good news though." She pecked his lips to start to brighten his attitude a bit.

"What? You got commission on a big sale?"

"Nope." She pecked his lips once more.

"You killed Davetta and Terry? Cherie, why would you be happy about that?"

"No, crazy ass." She rolled her eyes and kissed him one last time.

"Then tell me what it is. I need to know."

"You… De'Shane Hartford… are going to be a father again."

Shane removed her arms from his neck and took a sloppy step

back. There was a blank expression on his face that she couldn't decipher. "You're pregnant?"

"Yes, babe," she blushed. "We're finally going to be parents together!"

Shane picked her up and wrapped her legs around his waist. "Really, Rie? And it's mine?"

She smacked her lips. "Really? Of course, it's yours! Whose else would it be?"

"I'm just making sure, baby. We're really going to be parents?"

"Yes," she giggled. "On top of that, I didn't get a sonogram because I wanted you to see it with me."

Shane was at a loss for words. His hard work in every single area didn't go in vain. He earned the girl, built the house, proposed to the girl, and knocked her up. If he had an actual crown in that moment, Shane would've shined it and boasted on it.

Cherie broke their unexpected tongue-wrestling match when her phone blared from her purse. Shane put her on her feet so that she could rummage through the contents of her handbag and find her phone. She rolled her eyes once she saw who was calling.

"Yea, Davetta?" she answered.

"You called *me*. Don't get prissy."

"Look, we need to have a sit-down. Just me and you."

"When?"

"Tomorrow morning. It'll be brief, and the bill will be on me. I'll send you the address." Abruptly she hung up and shoved her phone back inside her purse.

"What about Mandy?" Shane asked her.

"Don't push your luck, Mr. Hartford. You're lucky that I'm seeing her. I'll speak to Amanda another time."

Shane caught Cherie before she could walk away, spun her around, and rubbed her stomach from behind. "In the meantime, what do my babies want to eat?"

"Whatever comes out of that kitchen," she said with a giggle. "Oh, and some Reese's."

"I can make that happen. After you speak with Davetta, we're going to see Bo tomorrow afternoon. He's having an accelerated treatment. I need to cook and get on the phone with some grief counselors to book him a few appointments."

"Thanks, babe."

"For?"

"Everything," she told him with a smile. "Now, get to cooking because I'm hungry. Even though it's all going to come right back up."

The two shared a laugh as Shane escorted her up to their bedroom.

CHAPTER FOURTEEN

Revenge Best Served

Eight years ago...

*C*herie shivered in the bathroom for the second month of her missing her period. She was only sixteen with what she thought would be the rest of her life ahead of her. Davetta banged on the door with force, startling the already frightened young woman. "Let's go before you're late, girl!" she screamed.

Hoping that Davetta would have some sort of mercy, she opened the door and stared at her mother with such a somber look that would break any normal person's heart.

"Fuck wrong with you?" Davetta asked her nastily.

"He's been taking me," Cherie lowly admitted. "I don't have my period yet, mama."

Davetta closely eyed her daughter in her pajama shirt that had thin shoulder straps on them and her loose-fitting pajama shorts. Of course, Davetta was highly envious of the curves that she developed even before her time. Davetta was built like a stick with small mounds here and there. She had no real waistline and no figure. Sometimes she would get the urge to make Cherie ugly in some way, which was the reason she beat her or called her nasty names.

Cherie anxiously awaited a response.

"He wouldn't want you, girl," Davetta spat. "Not when he has all of me lying in his bed. Your hoe ass has been runnin' around her with these little boys and don't know who the father is, so you want to blame it on my man?"

"Mama—"

Davetta grabbed Cherie by her long and thick auburn locks and slung her onto the hall floor. "You're getting that shit fixed!" she yelled. "You ain't gon' lay up in my man's house with a bastard in your belly! You hear me!"

Cherie bowed her head with her hand covering her face.

"You get every-fucking-thing that a princess deserves, but ain't no princess fuckin' the king of the castle to spite the hell out of the queen."

"He took me, Mama!" Cherie pleaded. "I didn't ask him to!"

Davetta hauled off and kicked Cherie in the chest, amid screaming, "Get the fuck up and go to your room! Gonna fuck around and claim you're pregnant by mine? Please. You ain't worth lookin' at, you lil' lyin' ass bitch! Don't try to compete with mother, baby, 'cause you ain't got it!"

In a hurry, hurt physically and emotionally, she got up and went to her room. In her bed, Cherie knew that something was going to have to give. But never did she think that Davetta would make her give up her only child.

———————

She didn't want to, but Cherie sat across from Davetta, who was chowing down on a Southwest salad like she hadn't eaten in awhile. Cherie smirked. She knew that the bills and the rent for the condo were eating Davetta alive. Her smile slowly faded when she remembered the day that Davetta made her walk into the clinic alone. The staff informed her that because she was underage, her mother would have to come back to be with her.

"I got to get to the sale at Macy's, Cherie!" Davetta yelled at her over the phone. "You make me miss this sale and it's gonna be hell in your world!"

While waiting on her mother that day, Cherie sat in the waiting room with her hand over her stomach, reminding her unborn of how sorry she was for what was about to happen. She promised her baby that she would see it again in heaven one day. After the procedure, Davetta carried on as if nothing had happened, yet Cherie saw what kind of soft side men had if they got the chance to experience a woman's sex. She turned something bad into somewhat of an advantage. Eventually, Davetta noticed what kind of attention Cherie was getting and how her so-called man was neglecting her, so they moved. The next victim, however, was a masculine woman. Davetta actually stood there one day and watched as her lover devoured her own daughter's breasts. She seethed. Again, they moved. This time, the man had a son and introduced the two. Thus, entering Terry into the picture. Two years of being with him, and she was pregnant again. A miscarriage due to being tossed down the steps for wearing red lipstick was inevitable. After which, Terry claimed that it wasn't meant to be there in the first place.

Cherie now ran her hand over the cotton fabric of her button-up with a small smile on her face. *This one is meant to be,* she thought.

"So, what's up?" Davetta asked as she dabbed a napkin at the corners of her mouth.

Cherie sighed. "First thing's first." Finally, Cherie took off her mirror tinted shades, properly folded them on the table, and placed her hands daintily over them. "I'm getting married; of course you know that. Now, I'm pregnant."

Davetta's head lightly tilted to the side. "Is it Shane or Terry's?"

"Why the fuck would it be Terry's?"

"Because you know that he's wanting you back."

"Listen, I wish you would stop thinking about money and think about everything else. But you know what? I don't fault you. That shit is rooted deep within you, Davetta. The blame lies with me. If I would've been as strong as I am now, then I wouldn't have let anything happen to me. I don't care how cruel you were as a mother, I should've been stronger to get away from it, or make it not affect me. This baby that I'm having will have a real mother. One who will tuck them in at night and won't have to chase a man just to live. They will be my priority. They won't be my meal ticket."

"Look, Cherie. We're not going back down this road."

"Of course we're not, dear. I thank you for the finer things that you exposed me to. I thank you for playing a helping hand in making me stronger. I thank you for showing me what a mother is not. I most definitely thank you for showing me who I don't want to be. Lastly, I thank you for giving me life and moving us close to Aunt Pat so that I would meet my fiancé. A real man. One who would stop at nothing just to make sure that his woman is taken care of and is comfortable."

"You're welcome," Davetta said smartly.

"One more thing. I love you, Davetta. Regardless of everything, I have a mother, even though sometimes I wish you would just roll over and die. I still love you after all the hoe ass shit that you've done. But don't you ever... reach out to me for a damn thing. Even though I love you, you're dead to me." With that, Cherie rose from her seat and tossed a hundred-dollar bill on the table for the check. Then, with her head held high, she left the restaurant altogether.

———

Soon, Cherie was standing on the doorstep of the bungalow where she spent plenty of nights eating and having fun for a change as a child. The door opened and her own cousin stood before her with wide eyes.

"Cherie?" Mandy said breathlessly.

Rudely, Cherie pushed herself inside the house and took a seat on the couch. Using what she learned from a finishing school that Davetta put her in using her producer girlfriend's money, she crossed her legs and placed her purse beside her.

"I... I like your cut," Mandy said nervously as she awkwardly wiped her hands off on her work pants. "What, umm…? What brings you by?"

"Don't try to act like everything that happened between us didn't happen."

"I'm not saying that it didn't. I just don't want to think about it."

"Have a seat, Amanda."

Cautiously, Mandy rounded the couch and sat on the edge of it, wondering what Cherie could've wanted.

"You know… this family is riddled with cowards, Amanda," Cherie began. "I just had a talk with your aunt, but I'm going to assume that you know that because y'all seem very close these days. For the life of me, I can't understand how you… my *favorite* cousin… my *ace* in this family, could sit around and gossip with my mama, whom you know that I can't stand. Not only that, but you kissed *my* man and withheld messages from me? Now, I would've expected that from *Davetta*. Not from *you*."

"Let me explain." Mandy rubbed her palms on the knees of her pants with her eyes on the coffee table in front of her. "I had a crush on Shane when we were younger. I thought you knew about it, but I guess you didn't pay attention. I mean, y'all were never together, so after you left, I started working on my chance. I tried to kiss him, he left, and we didn't see each other again until he met me in the waiting room the night that my mama passed. The next best thing was Rich. It's crazy to say, but I thought that he would be a little like Shane—"

"And you rooted on our relationship, why? In the back of your mind, you were hoping that I would fail?"

"No," Mandy whined. "It wasn't like that. I thought that I had another chance at being the friend and cousin to you that I was supposed to be, and I thought that in rooting you on, I could let my feelings for him go."

"You bitch." Cherie shook her head. "That was so fake of you, Amanda. I still can't believe that you would've done me like that. But you know what? Love… *real* love… will always prevail."

"Cherie, you had *everything*!" Mandy suddenly shouted. "You got expensive vacations, fine cuisine, name brand clothes—"

"That *I* paid for with my flesh and blood!"

"So? But you still got it! Meanwhile, I'm stuck here in this dump, never to fucking leave Richmond. Why? Why couldn't I deserve it all?"

"What the fuck did you do to so-call deserve anything?"

"Because before there was a Shane, there was me. *I* looked out for you. *I* cleaned up your cuts and covered your bruises. *I* fed you."

"Because that's what family does for one another!"

"And Shane? Why didn't I deserve someone who would wait on me hand and foot and give me everything he thought that I was deserving of?"

"Bitch, you had *Rich*! With how he treats Alyssa, there's no doubt in my mind that he treated you the same fucking way. You just had your sights on everybody else and what they were getting."

"I deserve—"

"To get your head out of your ass, you fake motherfucker! You were my blood and the only one that I've trusted. To know that you were so-called jealous of me hurts. You had no reason to be. When I came back home, I shared every-fucking-thing with you. I paid on the mortgage so that you wouldn't have to, you never paid for a meal, your utilities were covered, and bitch, I damn near restocked your fucking wardrobe! Because I had it, you had it. You let your feelings get in the way of so much, which makes you fake as fuck. But that's not why I came here. I came because Shane... you know, *my* man... wanted me to bury the hatchet with you. Consider it buried. I love you, I forgive you, and that's just it. Like Davetta, Amanda, you're dead to me."

With her mouth agape, she watched her cousin sashay away as if to seriously be saying goodbye.

———————

Finally, Cherie met Shane and the family in the parking lot near the Coleman Center. She got out of her car and approached the somber looking bunch. Once she was close enough, Shane fondly wrapped an arm around her shoulders and pulled her into the side of him. As a force of habit, her hand reached up to the chest of his white Polo.

"What's the matter?" she asked lowly.

As if her words struck a nerve, tears from the bottom of Shane's Ray Ban's, wet his cheeks. His face was still blank, but she knew that something was wrong.

Cherie looked to Joyce who had her face hidden on Erykah's shoulder. She leaned off her daughter and dabbed the corners of her eyes with tissue from her hand. "Bo..." Joyce tried. "He... bit his tongue last night."

"And then?"

"He bit a nice size off, Rie," Alyssa informed her. She was stroking Rich's back. The poor guy was broken down to his knees. "Lucky for him they stopped the bleeding in time. He's heavily sedated. They transferred him to the hospital last night and didn't fucking call the family to let us know a damn thing."

"No," she quietly gasped.

Shane lost the feeling of his legs. Like Rich, he was now on his knees, crying inside Cherie's stomach. She rubbed his back to keep him comfortable and to try and take away the pain. They hadn't had to plan a funeral in a while, and she knew how Shane hated to lose the ones he loved. He had come so far from being diluted and crazy. She didn't want him to end up back-peddling.

The group ended up going back to the Big House for dinner, and everyone tried their best to keep their heads clear. The only thing to put them all at ease was the call that came in on Rich's cell phone. Once he answered, a nurse informed him that Bo was now stable after a two-pint blood transfusion. She informed him that Bo would have to stay there for about another week so that they could oversee his recovery, but he would still be sedated. She promised to keep Rich updated day by day.

Afterward, Shane and Cherie were able to go back to their home without Miracle. Joyce insisted on keeping her. She told them that she wanted to keep her little hellish angel close. She said that she needed a little sunshine after all of the chaos.

Shane pulled into the garage and closed it. Immediately, his body tensed. He shut the car off with his lids narrowed.

"What's the matter, babe?" Cherie asked with a giggle. "My car is safe at the Big House. We'll go and get it in the—"

Her sentence was cut short by Shane opening the glovebox of the Jaguar. Out of it fell a twenty-two pistol with a chrome handle. He snatched it up and gave it to Cherie, but his eyes were still on the door that you could barely tell was cracked. "If you don't know how to use one of these, you better take a lucky guess."

"Babe, what—"

He shushed her. "If I'm not back in three minutes, you come in there and bust at anything moving, you hear me?"

Fear paralyzed Cherie. Involuntarily, she sat in the passenger seat shivering.

Shane only imagined her giving him a yes for an answer, and got out of the car to walk into his own home. Yes, he was strapped with a .50 caliber tucked in the waistband of his jeans behind his back, but he also had concealed firearms all over his house. Even Cherie knew this by her having to put them all back into their proper places when she redecorated the house.

With poise, calmness and a relaxed demeanor, Shane opened the door that wasn't supposed to allow entrance unless there was a thumbprint that had already been stored in the system. There were no police and no alerts to him that his system had been compromised. Whoever broke into his home must've known what they were doing. But who would be foolish enough to try to rob Shane tha God?

Casually he closed the door to the garage behind him and went to his island. To calm his nerves, he reached underneath the island and grabbed his brandy. Then, he opened a cupboard to get himself a glass. When he closed it. There was a silhouette of a man leaning against the entryway that didn't startle him. Thanks to his amazing sense of smell after his surgery, he remembered that loud cologne that Terry wore the night they came face to face before Shane's wedding. Terry was even wearing it when he pummeled the man to a bloody pulp.

He wasn't bothered and proved so with how he took a seat on the barstool at the island to pour his drink. "A man like you who got into my house somehow deserves a congratulatory drink after it. Come. Have a seat."

Shane heard the click of Terry's gun, but that still didn't stop him from sitting his brandy bottle on the island top or from taking a nice gulp of his drink.

"I like it dry," Shane said after swallowing.

"Why the fuck would I care?" Terry spat angrily.

"Because it seems you care about all the shit that doesn't concern you. I mean, you came to warn me to stay away from Rie when I was about to marry someone else. You took the time to come all the way out here to chop it up with Davetta about shit when she didn't concern you either. A man like you who wears five thousand dollar cufflinks cares too much about shit that you shouldn't."

A wicked smirk came across Terry's face as he leaned up from the pane of the entryway. "You know what I give a fuck about, De'Shane? I give a fuck that when I tried to fuckin' kill you the first time, it didn't work."

Shane's glass was almost at his lips when he had to retract it. His head slowly turned to Terry as a way to keep his cool. "Fuck are you talking about? Ain't nobody ever tried to kill me."

"Outside of your sister's beauty shop. You don't remember?"

His nostrils flared.

"I got the pictures back and rejoiced over the fact that Cherie was finally out of my goddamn hair. But… they left you a-fucking-live."

"What?"

"I know that everybody has a damn twin, but shit. You were one lucky motherfucker, weren't you? Davetta told me about her old lover's kid. How the girl and Cherie looked so much alike. It's a goddamn shame that it's your fault that she had to go before her time. See, I don't like to lose. To get a one-up on you, I came to pay you a little visit since you like to sit on the stairs in a motherfucker's house." Terry stopped across from Shane on the other side of the island, knowing that he stepped on a scar that would open up and gush blood. "I had to let you know before I put you out of your misery."

Even though Shane wanted to hop across the island and strangle Terry, he relaxed and brought his glass back up to his lips. "You see, the problem with you bad guys is that you talk too fucking much."

"Oh? And while I'm talking, let me just let you know that since I killed the wrong sister, I'll be there to console Cherie and raise both your kids like they're my own."

"Terry, shut up and shoot me," Shane said nonchalantly.

"What's the matter? The truth hurts too much?"

"No. You're going to fuck around and say something that's going to piss somebody off."

"Somebody like who?"

The sound of a gunshot cracked through the air like thunder. The small hole in Terry's black t-shirt was what got his attention instead of the pain. Slowly, he reached up to it and touched it. When the shock wore off and he realized that he had been shot, he turned to see who had shot him.

With all of the bullshit and fuckery that Terry and her mother put her through driving that first bullet through his chest, Cherie held the gun firmly in her hand with her purse in the other. Her eyes were cold and hard. Her hand was steady. He didn't receive any mercy from her.

"You shot me," Terry said breathlessly before he collapsed onto the floor.

Rage that matched Shane's couldn't be detained in that moment. Cherie had yet to be done with Terry for every time he had hit her. Every time he cheated. Every time he broke her spirit and treated her like she was nothing. Cherie had blacked out. She had long dropped her purse and was now beating Terry senseless with the back of the gun that Shane had given her in the car. There wasn't a single tear to escape her eyes. Even with a cramp in her arm, Cherie felt that what she was doing was not serving a justice.

Knowing that it was her first time using the handgun period, Shane took one more gulp of his brandy and went over to his fiancée to catch her arm. "We have to think of the baby, Rie," he said lowly. She didn't want to let it go, but Shane managed the gun from her strong fingers. Then, he helped her to her feet. Cherie hadn't moved a muscle. Her eyes were focused on Terry as he reached for the pistol that he dropped. As the gentleman he was, Shane placed the .22 on the island as he wrapped one arm around Cherie's waist, then reached for his .50 caliber behind his back. Before he drew it, he murmured, "Don't look, babe."

Cherie turned her head to bury her face inside his chest.

Waiting what seemed like forever to have this moment had already taken a toll on Shane. He aimed for Terry's head and fired off a round. Cherie flinched when she heard the gun go off. Then, with her face still hiding, Shane guided her out of the kitchen and up the stairs to their bedroom.

After seating her, he pulled his cell phone from his pocket. "Rich," he said after three rings. "Have a maid service come to the house, man. I have a big mess that needs to be cleaned up, but I can't clean it myself, and you know Cherie is still in the tender stages of having a weak stomach with this baby."

"What happened?"

"You know, unexpected visitors can sometimes turn into a wild party. I got wine stains on the marble in the kitchen. You know damn well I don't know how to clean that up."

"I got you. I'm gonna call someone."

Shane hung up and kneeled in front of Cherie.

Her darting eyes finally met his.

"Well, baby… that means that no one is going to protest at the wedding."

"Oh my god!" Cherie wailed, swatting at his arm. "Right now?" she asked with a laugh. "Seriously?"

"What?" He shrugged. "It made you laugh."

"And did you have to speak in code around me?"

"It wasn't for you, baby. That was in case somebody had my line tapped."

"Shane?" Cherie pouted.

"What, babe?"

"I'm hungry again."

"Right now, Rie?" His face contorted. "I expected you to be sad or confused. Not hungry."

"Look! I can't control my cravings! You're the one who wanted so badly to put this baby in me—"

"And you wanted that baby badly, didn't you? What am I supposed to say? Hi, Thai food delivery man! Can you come around the back? I kind of have a dead body on my kitchen floor right now?"

Cherie's face slowly morphed into a frown. Tears came at the drop of a dime. "Sometimes, I think that you just don't care!" She leaped off the bed and stormed off the bathroom, where she slammed the door and locked it.

"Rie!" he called after her. "Rie! Baby, I'm sorry!"

"No, you're not! And I don't even know why I'm crying!"

Shane dropped his head and focused on his breathing to keep

himself calm. "You wanted this, Shane. You act like you weren't around your first baby's mama when she was emotional for no reason. Oh, *and…* you wanted this one to marry you. Congratulations, dumbass."

"Don't make fun of me when I can hear you!" Cherie cried from the other side of the door. "You should be worried about the fucking body on the kitchen floor! Move his ass and make me my food! Don't nobody give a fuck about Terry!"

He shut his eyes tight and grabbed the bridge of his nose. "Yea, Shane. You wanted this shit."

"I can still hear you!"

He then looked over his shoulder and smiled. They had finally fit the groove of one another.

CHAPTER FIFTEEN

Tale As Old As Time

Bo gave Shane a fist pound and a hug after straightening his gold colored necktie. He couldn't speak, but Shane could tell that Bo was proud of him. It was in his eyes. Joyce came up behind Bo inside Shane's suite with a lent roller to make sure that nothing was on anyone's white linens. When their eyes met, she could see the dear friend that her late husband had always had in him. Since his treatment, Bo was on the straight and narrow. Shane even took precaution as to give sole responsibility of his father's dynasty to Rich and Alyssa without telling Bo. He even moved him to a different part of Richmond, just to make sure that his nose would remain clean. Shane even escorted him to his therapy sessions. His second father was present on his wedding day, alert and as happy as Apollo would be.

Joyce had given Bo a warm smile and patted his cheeks. "Let's get a move on, y'all," she said to the other men. "Baby, are you ready?"

Shane double-dutched in place to shake off his nerves.

"You ready?" Rich coached him as he slipped on his jacket. "I say, is you *is* or is you *ain't* ready to do this, Hartford?"

"Let's do this," Shane returned with a huff.

The two shared a familiar handshake, then Rich grabbed Shane's shoulders to massage them as his friend had gone bouncing. "Twelve years, dog."

"*Twelve*," Shane chorused.

"A baby mama, plenty of drama, bullshit and fuckery. You ready?"

"Ooh, all of that. I'm ready."

"Cherie's out there, boy."

"*Cherie!*"

"You're about to marry her."

"*Marry* her!"

"Got a baby on the way."

"The *baby*."

"You got to go out there, put that ring on her finger—"

"On the *finger*."

"—look her deep in the eyes, and say I do."

"'Cause I do!"

"Let's do this, son!"

As if he was about to go and play basketball, Shane finally stopped hopping up and down just to slap hands with his best friend.

Across the hall, Josiah kissed Cherie's cheek after Quita adjusted the crown that had a sheer white veil falling behind it. "Are you ready, Pumpkin?" he asked his daughter.

Happily, Cherie nodded as she hooked arms with her father.

Her dress made of delicate corded lace on tulle skim shoulders. The neckline of the lightweight gown had an attached Monroe slip dress while buttons trailed a zipper closure that was accenting a deep illusion back. Her train was also lace with white floral patterns commenting the embedded roses inside her golden crown. With class and elegance, she began her trip to the alter doors.

"Miracle?" Erykah called her. She waved the little one over so that she could grab her basket and chuck flowers over the white runner as she walked.

As expected, Miracle didn't walk. She ran and threw the gold rose petals to the ground, then climbed up on the platform where her father stood so that he could pick her up. With his hair braided in two fishbone cornrows, Shane grabbed up his daughter and rubbed his nephew's head at his side. Even King didn't do his job. He kept the Bible in one hand and the pillow that the Bible should've been on in the other. The music struck up and Shane's heart began to pound outside of his chest. He wasn't having an anxiety attack. He was just more than anxious to have this moment come true.

Before the doors of the church opened, Cherie closed her eyes and thought of their school project. In her backyard, she and Shane had a mock wedding just to be their own stand-ins so that they could take photos for her vision board. She remembered going over her lines in her head and promising to always belong to him. Cherie pulled the photo they took from her bra. She had snagged it when she found the blue binder she kept from that project and had stuffed it inside her bra to remind her of their own little story. It reminded her of how far they had come.

"Here we go, honey," Josiah whispered.

A smile instantly draped Cherie's face. She was finally taking the trip down the aisle. To represent the story of Aladdin and Jasmine, they had hanging doves to remind them of the magic carpet ride they took. To represent Mulan's story, the runner was of gold and white Chinese art. White and gold masks were placed on the edge of each pew as a taste of New Orleans to represent Princess Tiana and Prince Naveen. Her vision really did pull together.

As expected, Rich was standing in his rightful place as the best man. Even he had a beaming smile on his face. Joyce, however, couldn't stop crying since the doors opened for Shane to walk her and seat her on the front row. The sisters, standing on Cherie's side, kept having to dab away tears.

Cherie was trying her best not to shed a tear, but that fell through when Josiah had finally stopped her at the platform.

"Who gives this woman away?" the pastor asked.

"I do," Josiah said proudly.

Josiah guided Cherie's hand to meet Shane's, then he whispered something to the young man that was very personal. Not only was it a threat, but it was a solid promise that if Cherie ever called him and told him that she was hurt, that Shane might as well skip whole continents because he was going to come and find him with a sawed-off shotgun.

Shane smiled and nodded, knowing that he wouldn't dare hurt her any more than he already had. He then helped Cherie to step up on the platform and handed Miracle over to Joyce.

"Let us pray over this union," the pastor prompted everyone.

Tears streamed down Cherie's cheeks during the prayer. She wanted to shout out how much she couldn't believe that they had made it. Shane, standing firm and strong with a straight back, wanted to break out and dance. Yet, he kept it concealed. Besides, the women would have a fit if he somehow ruined the white tuxedo he wore with gold trimmings, or scuffed his white leather Italian loafers with gold steels tips on them.

"Amen," the congregation said in unison.

"If there is anyone here who thinks that these two should not be wed—"

Immediately, Rich and the other three groomsmen pulled back their white tuxedo jackets to showcase their guns at their sides, then casually stuffed their hands in their pockets as a solemn warning for no one to speak.

"—speak now or forever hold your peace."

Joyce fanned herself with one of the church's fans as she rocked back and forth with her granddaughter on her lap. "*Amen!*" she called when there was no one to stop the wedding.

"And now, may I have the rings please?"

Erykah handed Cherie the ring she chose for Shane. Shane reached behind him to retrieve the ring from Rich. A few seconds passed and there was nothing to be passed.

Shane turned to Rich.

"What you lookin' at me for?" Rich asked him.

"Where's the ring, bro?"

"I don't know. Am I supposed to have it?"

"Rich. Don't play with me right now, bro. I remember handing you the ring at the hotel yesterday morning."

"That memory loss is gettin' to you then because you didn't hand me nothin'."

"Rich. This is very important. Now give me the ring."

"I'm tellin' you that I ain't got it."

Shane rolled his eyes and turned to Cherie. He stared into her angry face, about to apologize and come up with another way to take his vows, when Rich slipped his hand through Shane's jacket and arm. Angrily, Shane snatched it and opened the box.

"Had to get you one more time, brotha," Rich whispered.

Behind his back, Shane gave him back the box. Along with it came his middle finger.

"I can see you," Joyce told him.

"Now, do you, De'Shane, take this woman to be your lawfully wedded wife?" the pastor asked him.

In a hurry and without thinking, Shane blurted, "I do."

"And do you, Cherie—"

"I do," she cut him off.

Together, they slipped on their rings with smiles that couldn't be tamed or wiped away.

"You may now—"

The pastor was cut off once again by Shane taking the sides of Cherie's face into his hands. Their faces drew close until Shane stopped.

"I want to kiss you so bad… but first—"

"Let me take a selfie!" Rich yelled as he jumped in front of them with his phone in his hands to take the picture. "Yea, that one's going on Instagram. Hashtag, BFF Life!"

"Y'all are so childish," Alyssa commented three sisters down from Cherie.

Cherie rolled her eyes as she turned to face her. "And this is why I never hung out with him alone."

"We had to annoy you one last time," Shane chuckled. "Come here, girl. I've waited twelve years for this moment."

Once their lips were sealed, that spark inside might as well had been fireworks the way they went off.

The two parted lips and took their walk down the aisle and to the front doors of the church that Erykah scouted. When they opened, the white doves that Cherie always wanted were released. They almost startled her.

"What do we do now, Mrs. Hartford?" Shane asked her.

"We should…" Cherie dropped her bouquet and grabbed her mouth. Then, she let Shane's hand go and rushed over to the rail to let go of all of her stomach contents.

"You got that?" Shane asked the photographer across the street.

The man with the camera in his hand gave him a thumbs up.

"Yea, this is going in your little blue binder, Rie."

"Shut up, Shane!" she cried.

His smile couldn't be bigger. He had married his best friend. Although everything was perfect, there was one more hurdle to jump over.

Six months later, Cherie was screaming louder than any other pregnant woman was allowed to. They were awaken at two in the morning by wetness on their bedsheets. While the family waited on the first floor, Joyce was on her knees behind Cherie who was sitting a blowup tub with her legs as wide as they could go. Shane had finally sat his camera on a tripod so that he wouldn't have missed a single moment of their first child coming into the world. He felt a little guilty and selfish, seeing as how he had done none of it for Miracle, yet he reminded himself that there were plenty of photos and videos of her in his memory cards from his sisters and mother recording them in his absence.

He stepped into the tub with his half-naked wife while she was trying her best to breathe. The back of her head lay on Joyce's shoulder. The doctor was circling the pool while coaching Cherie to breathe, yet she should've been coaching Shane.

His eyes were wide when he saw of a different color below the surface of the water. "Holy shit," he breathlessly said. "Oh my god."

"What?" Cherie managed through her labored breaths. "What's happening?"

"Babe… something's coming out."

"It's a baby!" Joyce screamed at him. "It's supposed to come out."

"No, like… ma… it's really coming out."

"It's supposed to," Cherie whined.

"Like this?"

"Quit!" Joyce hissed.

"Oh shit, mama it's coming!"

"Dad, put your hands forward," the doctor instructed him.

"Shane, get it out!" Cherie cried.

"I can't grab a baby's head and pull it!" Shane panicked. "What if I snap its neck? What if I paralyze its for the rest of its life?"

Joyce leaned over and smacked her son's neck. "Stop all of that!" she urged him. "You lean forward and get ready to catch your child, De'Shane Hartford! Stop being a pussy!"

With a dropped jaw and frowning face, he did as he was told.

The wail that Cherie let out alerted everyone on the block that she was down to her last two pushes. She bore down, gritted her teeth and pushed as hard as she could without listening to the other three in the room who were sharing their comments and encouragement.

The only thing that made her open her eyes was the sound of the sloshing water, and Shane announcing, "It's a boy!"

She looked at the pair, at Shane's smile and misty eyes in particular. She had done it. She had finally brought a baby into the world that was all her own.

"We have a boy, Rie," Shane said with the newborn cradled in his arms. "Oh, man. He has my nose. Yea, he'll want a nose job very soon."

"Shut up," she whined.

Casually and gently, he handed their new bundle of joy off to Cherie. Her happiness was too much to contain. Cherie skipped the stages of frowning, moaning and gradually letting her volume rise. She went straight to bawling. She cried with her shoulders shaking. "You're beautiful," she cried to her brand new baby boy. "You're here and you're so beautiful. I have a son, and you're mine."

"What will you name him?" Joyce asked over Cherie's shoulder with tears wetting her cheeks.

"He'll be a second. De'Shane Hartford the Second."

"I have a Deuce?" Shane was astonished. "Really? You're giving me a Junior?"

"I am. We're not going to call him either of those names, but I have given you something that you once gave me."

"What's that?"

"Life, Shane. You gave me *life*."

Finally, Cherie took her eyes off of their son and looked up at him with a smile. Their journey to love and happiness was finally complete.

Within thirty minutes, Shane had helped Cherie to shower after the doctor checked her insides to make sure that everything was intact, and had properly surveyed and record everything about the baby. He helped his wife into a long gown so that Joyce could finish with oiling her skin and making sure that her daughter-in-law was protected from the heavy bleeding that would follow. She also escorted Cherie to the bed where Shane had pulled back the covers before retrieving the rest of the family. Once Cherie was in bed and had the covers over her midsection, Joyce handed her a bottle that she warmed up from Cherie's collection of milk that she had so far.

"Baby! Baby!" Miracle cheered from her father's arm.

"Yes, he's a baby," Shane chuckled as they entered the room.

"My baby."

"No, not your baby, Ren. He's your brother."

Miracle placed her hands on her father's cheeks to make him look at her. "*My* baby, daddy."

"Fine, bossy. He's your baby." Shane placed Miracle in the bed beside Cherie and was still in awe at how they finally had a baby. To him, Cherie was gorgeous there with his namesake in her arms.

Miracle used Cherie's shoulder to climb up so that she could get a better look at her new brother. "His name Shane, mommy," she said.

"It is," she quietly giggled.

"I want my baby."

"You're going to have to wait until he's done eating. It's his first time."

"He gets chicken tonight!"

"No, Miracle. He doesn't have teeth."

"Oh." She then reached his cap to run her fingers over the fine knitting that Joyce had done when creating it. "Hey, Shane. My name Miracle. You're my new baby."

The moment was one that made Cherie's heart swell with joy. To

Stuck On You 2

add on to it, Shane crawled into bed and wrapped his long, muscular arms around his little family, planting a gentle kiss on Cherie's cheek. Closing her eyes forced the new set of tears to scroll her cheeks.

Joyce reentered the room with the rest of the family in tow. There were more hybrids of smiles with frowns and even more tears as they all gushed at the new addition.

"Man, Shane," Rich commented with his head tilted to the side. "He has your nose, bruh. That's voodoo."

"My baby doesn't have a bad nose," Cherie said with a sniffle. "I'm talking about the old one, not the new one. But even his nose isn't bad." She then kissed her little one's forehead.

Shane unwrapped his arms from around the other Hartford's and sat up on the side of the bed. "While you're talkin', when are you and Lyssa gonna give mama some more grandkids?"

Rich awkwardly scratched the back of his neck.

"For your nosy information," Alyssa responded as she wiped her tears away, "we're getting there. We want to be on the same page, is all."

"Don't even think to look over here," Quita told him with a smile. "I have three kids now, who aren't mine, that are just fine for me."

Erykah gave her a high five. "After what I went through to bring King in... I'm not havin' no more. He better grow up happy being the only child."

"Well..." Ashington lowly said. All heads turned to her in the corner near the head of the bed on Cherie's side. "I've kind of wanted to tell you guys... I'm having one soon."

204

The family started to reprimand her for telling such tall tales, yet she opened her bubble coat to showcase the stomach that she had been doing very well at hiding.

"Erykah!" Shane called as he rose off the bed. "How could you let this happen?"

"*Me*?" she squealed, pointing to herself.

"Yea, you! You were supposed to be watching her!"

"It's not my fault that she went and opened her legs!"

"You were over the girls! We had a solid agreement!"

"What was I supposed to do? Stitch her legs shut?"

The rest of the argument, along with the other members putting in their two cents, fell upon deaf ears to Cherie. She smiled at her baby and leaned in to rub their noses together. "This is your family now, Little Shane. You'd better get used to the noise. Mommy has."

The baby opened his eyes to show his mom that his peepers were a swirl of green and brown, just like hers. He also had Shane's natural scowl.

"You're just perfect."

THE END

"For DeAnn..."

CONNECT WITH SUNNY!

Twitter & Instagram: @imthatgiovanni

Tumblr: knojokegio.tumblr.com

Google Plus: Sunny Giovanni

Facebook: https://www.facebook.com/thesunnygiovanni/

OTHER ROYAL RELEASES FROM SUNNY

Chosen: A Street King's Obsession

Chosen 2: A Street King's Obsession

Chosen 3: A Street King's Obsession

Givana & Slay: A No Questions Asked Love Story

A Forbidden Street King's Love Story

*A Forbidden Street King's Love Story 2:
Through Hell & High Water*

Love & Cocaine: A Savage Love Story

Love & Cocaine 2: For Better or Worse

Stuck on You: Shane & Cherie's Story

Stuck on You 2: Shane & Cherie's Story

Stuck on You 3: Shane & Cherie's Story

Obsessed with a Savage

Caught Between Two Street Kings

Text ROYALTY to 42828 to join our mailing list!

To submit a manuscript for our review, email us at
submissions@royaltypublishinghouse.com

Text RPHCHRISTIAN to 22828 for our
CHRISTIAN ROMANCE novels!

Text RPHROMANCE to 22828 for our
INTERRACIAL ROMANCE novels!

Do You Like CELEBRITY GOSSIP?

Check Out QUEEN DYNASTY!
Visit Our Site: www.thequeendynasty.com

Get LiT!

Download the LiTeReader app today and enjoy exclusive content, free books, and more

CPSIA information can be obtained
at www.ICGtesting.com
Printed in the USA
LVOW07s1819110817
544663LV00011BA/674/P

BCPL
Baltimore County
Public Library

9 781546 566601